Crossing the Rubicon II
Semper Fi
(Always Faithful)

A book

by

R. C. Richter

Copyright © 2013 R. C. Richter

R. C. Richter
http://www.rcrichter.com/

Front cover and map illustration design by
Jirka Väätäinen
http://www.jirkavinse.com

Interior layout and art design by
Naïma van Esch
www.naimavanesch.com
Spanish language translation and editing by
Morella Villalobos
morella@shaw.ca
&
Brigitte Soulier
brisoulier@gmail.com

ISBN-13: 978-1492224426
ISBN-10: 1492224421

The *Crossing the Rubicon* series was first envisioned back in 1992, when my friends and I first explored the Chungo Caves. It was a story that would take twenty years to bring to print. Like the characters in this book, who each day struggle to survive, they make a point never to give up.
Semper Fi is the next book in the series and once again carries on the drive to live, to make the next hill. If you have a dream, a purpose, never let go. See it to the end.

ACKNOWLEDGMENTS

I want to thank the incredible group of people who were part of this project, plus those who found time to help in reviewing this book and making it the very best it could be.

I also want to thank my awesome family, to whom this book is dedicated, for the love, support, and inspiration you have given me during this amazing journey of writing Crossing the Rubicon II: Semper Fi.

To my loving wife, Sandra J. Richter, for her countless hours of proofreading and editing to make this project come to fruition.
Thank you, to Kalpit Momaya for helping with the film version of Crossing the Rubicon "The Journey"

To Jirka Väätäinen and Naïma van Esch for bringing my characters to life through their brilliant artwork, which is such an integral part of this book. To Morella Villalobos, for her time editing and ensuring that the Spanish translations in the book were done accurately. And a heartfelt thanks to Bill Biko for his out-of-the-box thinking, his thoughts and insights on the project, his creation of our online presence with Facebook, YouTube, and the website, and who made me almost wear out the phrase "great work, Bill" in my e-mails with him.

www.BillBiko.com

DEDICATION

This book is dedicated to Trinity, Bianca, and Erich.
As well as to my mother and father, Erika and Erich.
May you continue to follow your dreams, never give up, and always
see things to the end.

CONTENTS

PREFACE

Fifteen years ago, we found ourselves in this time in space. We had crossed the Rubicon. We were like aliens from a far-off world whose spaceship had crashed here high in the Canadian Rockies. All we had was the clothes on our backs and the few supplies we could salvage. That was how we felt about ourselves most of the time. For us, all that remained were our iPhones, the portal to who we were, and a few other tools from 2014. For us, our spaceship was a cave in a mountain, now so far away from our final stop and home here on La Palma, the Canary Islands. Our spaceship was now lost and forgotten. We would never return home to our own time and place in the universe. The door to 2014 was closed. All that remained now was the year 1754 and the life we had made for ourselves here.

I think back to how things were, who we were, who I was back then. So much I took for granted each day. Never once did I stop and thank those around me for all they did for me, for what they gave me. For this I will forever be burdened. It will eat at me until I leave this world for the last time.

I think back to my dad. Now, fifteen years later, I see him for who he was, a great man who did so much—not just in his life, but for me, my sisters and my mother. He loved me so much, a love I was never able to reciprocate.

I am reminded of when I was fifteen years old, my dad came home one day with a new Suburban 4x4 truck. To him it was new, but in fact, it was three years old already. He had purchased it from a person he knew in the US government. It was black, with a front bumper bush guard and tinted windows all around. It was like something the CIA or Secret Service would drive around in. Knowing my dad, most likely that was where he got it from. He told my mom it was for the family. After all, there were five of us, and he would sooner die than drive around in a minivan. I think back and still remember how opposed my parents could be at times. He had his big black Suburban, and my mom would park next to him with her small white Audi station wagon. Neither would drive the other's vehicle.

What is so key to this memory is not the black Suburban, but the red-and-gold plate that was on the front bumper. Most people would have a vanity plate made up, say, a flag or some interesting acronym that meant something important to them. But my dad's plate was a red background, with a gold crest on it, and the words "Semper Fi" below. One day I asked him about the plate and what it meant. He told me it was a gift from a Marine Corps colonel he knew in the United States. The crest on the plate was the Marine Corps logo, a globe with a ship anchor behind it, and an eagle sitting atop of the world. I remember asking him one cold fall morning, as he was scraping ice from the windows, what the words "Semper Fi" meant? He stopped and looked at me, and after a long pause, he said, "'Always faithful,' Trinity."

That is how I will always remember my dad, always faithful to the end. I wish I could say the same about myself. The pain I still feel for not being able to say good-bye to them continues to live with me each day. When someone dies, they are gone. Kim, Robert, they are gone, and I go on with life hoping that somehow, someday we will be united again. But, my parents are not dead. They live. Just not in our time. All that is left are a few poor photos of them standing in the background of family get-togethers, which I store on my iPhone. Again, there are more photos of my friends than of them. How I long to somehow reach out across space and once again touch them one last time. I so want to be always faithful to them.

Semper Fi, Mom, Dad. Someday my words will find you.

Chapter One

Dawn

August 20, 1754

The sun broke over the mountain volcano of Caldera de Taburiente, which towered a thousand metres (three thousand feet) high in the centre of La Palma Island. The morning air was cool; the wildlife of the island began its morning call.

Next to the sea, with a commanding view of the world around it, was the Kennedy estate, home, its white three-story seaside walls with tiered balconies towering high over the coastline. Just off from the centre of the home was a fourth story, a tower that gave the residents a 360 view of the countryside around. The home was capped with red roof tiles. The morning sun began to bathe the house in a brilliant golden-yellow light. The sea below rolled in gently as the waves washed onto the black sands that made up the coastline of the island.

Today, like every day on La Palma, the weather would be perfect. Not too hot and not too cool, a perfect twenty-six degrees Celsius.

Offshore in the distance was a small twin-masted sailing ship at anchor. It gently rolled in the waves as the sea birds flew high in the sky, circling it. In the master bedroom of this great villa, which overlooked the sea below from the open windows, Trinity and Jacob slowly awoke. The white netting that hung over their bed softly moved in the morning breeze.

Jacob rolled over and softly brushed the hair from Trinity's face. It revealed an older Trinity. She was now thirty-four years old. Her long brown hair ran down the length of her body. She was still as beautiful as she was at twenty-one.

Jacob leaned forward and kissed her. "Good morning," he said.

There was a knock at the master bedroom door, followed by "Buenos días" from the hall outside.

"Buenos días, Cristina," replied Jacob.

Trinity's eyes slowly opened as she looked up at Jacob. She smiled at him, as she had for the last fifteen years.

"Good morning," Trinity said as she stretched.

The door to the bedroom swung open as Cristina walked in with breakfast for the two. She placed the large tray down on a small side table and moved to open the drapes to let in the morning light.

"Gracias," Jacob said.

"Con gusto," replied Cristina.

Trinity and Jacob slowly sat themselves up in bed as Cristina took the tray out onto the stone-tiled balcony and placed it on a wood table.

"Gracias," Trinity said as Cristina returned inside.

Cristina smiled as she left the room, closing the doors behind her.

Jacob kissed Trinity one more time, then rolled over and left the bed to get dressed. Trinity sat there looking at him, and then looked out toward the open doors that led to the balcony.

Trinity stood and pulled on a morning robe and walked out onto the balcony, across the tan-colored tile floor, and stopped at the stone railing. She looked down at the sea below and then up at the birds. Her hair danced in the wind. Jacob walked onto the balcony, pulled back a chair, sat down, and began to pour the morning tea for Trinity and himself.

"What are your plans for today?" asked Trinity.

"Sorry?"

"Will you be out all day or back for lunch?"

"No, I'll be out all day in the fields with the workers; you won't see me until dark," replied Jacob.

Trinity sat down across from Jacob and began to drink her tea.

"What are your plans today?" Jacob asked.

"I have a meeting with the staff to discuss some of the repairs that need to be done on the estate and then I'll see what the kids want to do."

"That is if you can get them up."

"They'll get up. They have lessons today with the friar."

Trinity looked at Jacob.

"What? Something wrong?"

"No. Just thinking how lucky I am," Trinity said.

"Ditto, dear."

Jacob finished his bread and stood up. "I have to go, long day." He moved around the table and kissed Trinity. "See you tonight."

With that, he made his way into the bedroom, grabbed a few more clothes, and left for the day. Trinity sat there, gazing out at the sea as she sipped her tea.

In time, Trinity dressed and made her way down the curved stairs that led to the main floor of the house. The house was alive with staff moving about, doing the many chores required for maintaining their beautiful home. As Trinity arrived at the front door, she was just on time to see Jacob ride off on his white horse followed by a number of other field workers. The morning sun now swept across the courtyard and onto Trinity's face.

From behind her came Christopher, their nine-year-old son, a good-looking boy with bright brown eyes and wavy brown hair, who stood at around three feet six inches. He was tall, much taller than the other children his age in this time.

"Buenos días Maná" he said.

"Good morning, Christopher," Trinity replied.

With that, Trinity turned and took his hand, and the two headed back into the house.

As morning turned to afternoon, Trinity changed into riding clothes and made her way down the hall and up a set of narrow stairs to the tower lookout, which was the highest point of the house. She unlocked the heavy wood door and entered the round room, which was about fourth feet in diameter, and worked her way through the maze of desks, tables, and chairs to the far side. The room held the last of the treasures from the year 2014. On a large wood desk in the centre of the room sat a small wooden box with seven sets of initials engraved into it. Around it was a number of letters and notes, maps, and a small monocular. Trinity stopped and picked up a stack of papers she was working on. On the cover, the words "Crossing the Rubicon" were scribed: below it, "With Love."

Trinity placed the sheets down and made her way to a small bookshelf ladder on the far end of the room and began to climb. It led to a ten by eight inch secret door above the bookcase, by the ceiling. As she pushed the door open, it revealed a small space with a glass window that replaced one of the red roof tiles above it. There, sitting on a small stone shelf, was an iPhone in a SLXtreme case, the solar panel facing the open sky so that the light of the sun would charge the unit each day.

Trinity reached in and pulled out the small orange case. It had become worn and beaten over the years. A leather strap bound the case together, protecting the knowledge it held inside. The case had cracks and marks all over it. Fifteen years of use had taken its toll. She took it and held it for a minute, checked that it had power, and then put it into a saddlebag with a set of earbuds. She then closed the small door, re-treaded down the ladder, and left the room, locking the door behind her.

By mid-afternoon, Trinity was riding her white horse along the beach, the black sand being kicked up by the horse's hooves. Her long hair blew in the wind as she picked up speed while the waves crashed inland as she galloped by. .

She finally came to a spot on the beach where, off on the hillside, there was a set of narrow steps that led up from the beach, into the rocks. She stopped, jumped down, and tied up the horse. Taking the saddlebag, she started to climb the narrow stairs up into the hills. After a few minutes, she reached a small clearing that had a table and a few chairs around it. Next to it was a number of long reclining chairs. There Trinity sat, kicking back and relaxing; she took the small orange iPhone case out and plugged in her earbuds. She then pulled out a set of beaten-up sunglasses, put them on, and lay back in her chair, pulling her hat over her face to protect it from the sun.

She turned on the iPhone and started to look for the right piece of music to listen to, finally settling on something that brought her peace as she played it. She lay back and closed her eyes. The wind in her face. The sounds of the waves below. Peace, joy, a time to escape, to be free— and perhaps in her mind, home again.

Trinity had lain there for almost an hour when there was a sound she had not heard in fifteen years. A ping sound? At first she didn't pay any attention, and then a minute later, there it was again. This time she looked up and then down at the iPhone case. She dropped her sunglasses and looked over them. Then again, a third ping. She sat up in the chair, picked up the iPhone case, and looked at it. On the main lock screen was a phone number of 000-000-0000 and a message: *Hello, Trinity.*

"What the hell?" she said.

She unlocked the iPhone screen and looked up in the top corner of the display. It showed that the phone now had a Wi-Fi connection.

Another message came across: *Trinity, are you there?*

Trinity looked around at the hills behind her. She then called out, "Jacob, quit screwing with me." She stood and looked around. "Jacob, what the hell? How are you doing this?"

5

Again the texted message came in: *Trinity, are you there?*

Trinity looked at the phone and then started to type: *Who is this?*

Trinity waited. Then: *Trinity, look at the sea. Do you see the ship at anchor?*

Trinity looked out at the sea and saw a double-masted sailing ship at anchor just to her right, below where her home was. She stood and walked to the edge of the cliff, looking at the ship.

Then from the ship there was a flash of light from a mirror.

The next message read: *Do you see my light?*

Trinity looked down and read the message and then responded: *Yes, who is this?*

The reply was: *Can I come ashore and meet you?*

Once again Trinity typed: *Who are you? What do you want?*

My name is Markus Keel. Please let me come and meet you at your home. I will explain everything once we meet face-to-face.

Trinity dropped the phone by her side and once again looked out at the open sea and the sailing ship. She grabbed her saddlebag, stuffed the iPhone into it, and then started to run down the long set of steps leading to the sea below. Trinity untied her horse and started to ride off down the beach as fast as she could. The water sprayed up as the horse raced toward the estate home and finally cut inland and up into the hills.

Twenty minutes later, Trinity rode up to the open gates of the estate courtyard. She jumped down from her horse and ran into the house. As she entered the main entrance, she called out to Felipe, the head of the household.

"Felipe!" She ran through the house looking for him. "Felipe, ¿dónde estás!"

From the kitchen, Felipe came. "Sí?"

"Busquen a Jacob, ahora!" Trinity screamed. "Get Jacob now!"

Felipe was shocked. He backed up and started to run from the house, calling to other men in the courtyard to get on their horses and ride out to get Jacob from the fields.

Trinity turned and ran to the main balcony, which led off from the study. As she stepped onto the balcony, the afternoon sun blinded her. She tried to look out at the open sea and the ship at anchor. As she stood there looking, she was just able to make out a small rowboat making its way toward the shore below the estate home.

"Oh my God! Oh my God!" Trinity looked around. She did not know what to make of all this. The world was starting to spin before her.

She then ran into the house and up the stairs, which finally took her once again to the tower room high atop the house. There, from the desk, she grabbed the monocular that Jacob had saved from half of the binoculars he once had. She made her way out a side door that led to an open-air balcony, which worked its way all around the tower like what one would find on a lighthouse.

Trinity walked to the ocean side and, using the monocular, looked down at the sea, searching for the small boat and the mystery passenger.

She finally found it just as it came ashore. From it stepped one man wearing a long black jacket with tails. He had on a hat, which blocked Trinity's view of his face. The man said his good-byes to the other four men in the boat, started to walk inland, and finally disappeared below the cliff.

Trinity slowly turned and stepped back into the tower room. There she stood, looking at all the things around her. Slowly she placed down the monocular and ran her hand across the top of the desk, touching many of the papers before her.

From the saddlebag around her shoulder she pulled out the iPhone and looked at it. She turned it on and once again started to look at the photos it held. She sat down by the desk and moved her finger across the screen, brushing each photo across to the next. One after another they moved across the screen. Before her was her life, the last fifteen years of it. There she sat for the longest time.

Her children passed by, photos of their home there on La Palma being built, Africa, the Orange River, the days at sea, and finally the photos of Kim Wong, the last day she saw her alive aboard the *San Ignacio*, the day the British attacked and the day she perished.

There was a knock at the door.

"Mam á puedo entrar?" Bianca said from out in the hall.

Trinity looked up, turned off the phone, and placed it in the small wood box sitting on the desk.

"What is it, Bianca?"

"Mam á, there is a man downstairs who wants to see you."

Trinity made her way over to open the door. Standing in the hall was Bianca, Trinity's thirteen-year-old daughter.

Bianca was five feet five inches, with long dark brown hair, and in every way her mother. She wore a cool white dress, with lace around the edges. A red sash finished the attire.

"Where is your father?" Trinity asked.

"He is still not back from the fields."

"I see."

"Who is the man?" Bianca asked.

"I don't know, Bianca. Let us find out."

Trinity and Bianca started to walk downstairs.

Chapter Two

The Gatekeeper

There standing in the main entrance hall of the estate was a tall man who looked to be in his early forties. A slender man, with the start of grey hair showing, he wore glasses, but not the glasses of this era, glasses more like the ones Jacob wore from the year 2014, frameless. In his right hand, he carried a black bag. As Trinity and Bianca entered the main hall, they saw Christopher standing next to the man, talking to him.

"Christopher, what are you doing?" Trinity asked.

"Mother, I am just making my introductions to our guest. He tells me his name is Markus Keel."

Markus looked over at Trinity and took off his hat. He smiled at her.

"It is still to be determined if he is a guest," Trinity said.

Christopher looked at his mother and then at the man standing next to him. "Mother?"

"Bianca, Christopher, can you please leave us? Go have dinner."

"What about you?" asked Bianca.

"I have business with…Markus." Trinity paused. She turned to Cristina, who was standing off to the side, watching. "When Jacob returns from the fields, tell him to join us in the study."

Cristina bowed and stepped back. Bianca and Christopher looked at their mother and then turned and left the hallway, leaving only Trinity and Markus looking at each other. There was a long pause. No one said anything. Finally Markus spoke.

"I have come a long way to meet you. You have no idea how hard it was to find you. We always thought you settled on Gran Canaria. It wasn't until last year that I found out you were on La Palma."

Trinity just stood there, not knowing what to say.

"I believe this is the way to the study?" Markus pointed and then stepped forward past Trinity.

"Sí…I mean, yes," Trinity said.

Markus gestured. "Would you like to lead the way? There is a lot I want to talk about."

Trinity took the lead, and the two made their way into the main study, just off of the balcony area. The sun was now low in the sky, the golden glow reflecting off the waves.

"I believe this is your favourite time of the day. Sunset," Markus said.

Trinity smiled.

"Please have a seat. Should we wait for Jacob? Or should I tell you who I am before he gets here?" Markus asked.

Trinity and Markus sat down opposite each other across a small table, each seated on their own long, embroidered couch. Trinity didn't take her eyes off him. him.

The sound of men yelling could be heard outside as a man rode up. A horse came to a quick stop. Then Felipe yelled out in Spanish for the staff to move out of the way. The main doors of the estate swung open, and Jacob entered into the great hall. He paused and then looked down the hall to find Trinity and Markus sitting in the study. Jacob took off his hat, dropped it on a side table, and marched into the study.

"Trinity, what's going on? I rode as fast as I could, but Felipe and his men had a hard time finding me."

"Jacob, it's all right! Enough," Trinity said, calming him down with a hand gesture.

Jacob looked at the stranger sitting in his study. He slowly moved around the back of the room to face Markus.

"Buenas tardes señor," Jacob said.

"Please, please no Spanish. My Spanish is not very good. I have tried these past few years to learn with little luck. So to keep the conversation going, can we speak in English?"

Jacob was caught off guard. "Yes, I can't see why not."

"Great!" Markus slapped his hands down on his knees. "I bet you have a lot of questions?"

Jacob turned and looked at Trinity. "I'm sorry, have I missed something here?"

"Yes, you see Markus…uh…"

"Keel. My last name is Keel. It's German."

"German? What do you mean German? You mean Germania."

"No, I mean German as in Germany," Markus responded.

"What the hell is going on here?" Jacob asked.

Trinity jumped in. "Jacob, Markus here sent me a text message on the iPhone."

Jacob looked at Trinity. "What?"

"I sent her a text message, this afternoon, asking to meet you here tonight. Took me a while to track and then log in to your phone. But luckily you left on your Wi-Fi, which made it possible. If not, we would not be sitting here now."

Jacob looked to Trinity, then back to Markus. "Who are you? And why are you here?"

Markus stood and started to walk behind the couch Trinity and Jacob were sitting on, toward a painting which was in the works of being finished. It was partly covered with a white sheet. He paused and then turned to Trinity and Jacob.

"May I?" he asked, pointing to the painting.

Trinity nodded in approval.

Markus pulled the sheet, revealing a six-by-eight-foot painting, 80 percent finished, of Trinity, Jacob, Bianca, and Christopher. In the painting, Trinity smiled as she sat in a chair with Jacob's hand on her shoulder; the two children, Bianca and Christopher, were by their parent's side.

Markus lifted his hands in surprise. "Awe, there it is. You have no way of knowing how special this work is, or will be, to your mothers and fathers!"

"OK, enough! Who the hell are you?" Jacob demanded.

Markus turned and looked at Trinity and Jacob. He gave a long sigh. "Like you, I am a time traveller."

Trinity and Jacob didn't know what to say. They were shocked. Jacob looked down the hall to see if any of the staff were nearby.

"What? You don't believe me? If anyone should, it should be you."

"But how?" Trinity asked.

"But how, indeed. You see, Trinity, Jacob, it is because of you and the message you sent, or will send, to your family in the future that we, that is we Gatekeepers, figured out the secret behind time travel."

Trinity was about to speak.

"Let me finish. You are going to ask how. Well, you gave us a date, an exact date. An exact date when you left in your time and an exact date when you arrived where you went to. Never before in all of history was this documented."

Jacob sat down next to Trinity.

"I have so much I want to tell. How and why. But, I think you should send a rider to Tom and Keara's home, asking them to join us. I think they, too, will want to hear what I have to say."

Trinity and Jacob just continued to sit on the couch. Finally Jacob said, "Yes, I think that would be wise."

"Good, shall we say meet for dinner in two hours from now? I am starving; I have not eaten since this morning. The whole thought of meeting you took my appetite away."

"Two hours should be enough time," Trinity said.

"Good, do you have room for a traveller such as me, a place I can rest and clean up?"

Trinity called out to Cristina and asked her to prepare dinner and to send a rider to invite Keara and Tom. Cristina asked if the children would be joining them.

"Not tonight," Trinity replied. "Not tonight."

Cristina turned and left the room, searching out the needed help.

"I will show you to your room," Trinity said.

"Thank you. I am sorry, but this is the only change of clothes I have for tonight. I trust they will be OK?"

Trinity looked at the man. "I think so. I think the story you will tell us will more than make up for how you are dressed."

With that, Markus picked up his black bag, and with Trinity and Jacob by his side, he was escorted out of the study and to his room for the night.

Dinner was served at nine that night. In the grand dining room, the food was laid out across a long table. Candles burned brightly as Trinity, Jacob, Tom, and Keara entered and made their way to their respective seats.

"Sorry, Trinity, tonight you're pissing us off. What gives with calling us over here like we are some house staff? It's late, dark, and I do not like riding a horse in the dark!" Keara snapped.

"Sorry, Keara, Tom. But there is someone you need to meet."

"What, it couldn't wait until morning?"

Jacob stepped in. "Ah, trust what Trinity is saying. It couldn't. After tonight, nothing will be the same again."

Keara stopped and looked up at Tom, who was pulling back a chair for her to sit. Tom looked down at Keara with a questioning look.

Just then, Markus made his entrance.

"Oh, I am so sorry I am late. I fell asleep and just woke up a few minutes ago. Sorry, but now I feel like, how you say…crap." He shook his head, trying to get a better feel for his senses.

Keara and Tom looked over to Markus.

"Keara, Tom, I would like to introduce you to Markus Keel," Trinity said.

Tom was about to sit, but then stood again to address the man.

"Please sit. Let's eat. I'm starving," Markus said.

"Yes, well, based on what you told us over two hours ago, I kind of lost my appetite. How about you, Jacob?" Trinity asked.

"Oh, well…do you mind if I eat? The food looks excellent!" Markus added.

Trinity gestured for Cristina and the other staff to start serving the food. One by one, the remainder took their seats. Trinity was at one end of the table, with Jacob at the far other end, and Keara, Tom, and Markus in the middle.

Markus dug in as the food was served. "Mmm, this is exquisite!" He took one more bite and then turned to Cristina. "Por favor déjeme decirle que esto es excepcional!"

Cristina smiled. "Gracias."

Keara and Tom looked at each other, a look of "What the hell is going on?" written all over their faces.

"Could I have some wine, please?" Markus asked, lifting his glass high, shaking it.

Trinity rolled her eyes. A house staff member stepped forward and poured him a glass of red wine.

"You live like kings; we do not eat this well on the ship," Markus pointed out.

"Enough!" Trinity snapped, banging the table. She turned to Cristina and the other staff and ordered them out. "Por favor déjenos." She now turned her attention to Markus. "You come into our lives, telling us you are a time traveller, and then you jerk our chain like this. How dare you!"

Keara and Tom almost choked on their food. "What?" Keara said.

"Sorry, Keara, Tom. Mr. Keel here is a time traveller, and he has come from the future with a message for us."

Tom and Keara looked at each other, lost for words.

"Well, not really, more a warning." Markus put down his utensils and looked to Keara and Tom sitting across from him. "No, you heard right. I am a time traveller, just like you all are. But, unlike you, I can pick my time and place when and where to travel. Well, more or less, there are a number of rules, or should I say limitations, we have to work around." Markus looked to his captive audience. "Sorry, I am being an ass. You've been here for, what, fifteen years now since you entered the cave?"

"How do you know that? Keara asked.

"Let us head up to your tower room so we can talk with no one interrupting us. I trust none of your house staff speaks English."

"No, they understand very little. Trinity and I make a point to speak Spanish around them. After all, it is their country," Jacob said.

Markus pushed back his chair. "OK, lead the way, Trinity."

Slowly they all stood and started to leave.

A short time later, they found themselves each sitting in the round tower room atop the estate home, Markus front and centre. Trinity and Jacob to one side and Keara and Tom to the other side, they waited for him to speak. Markus stood and looked out the window at his ship at anchor. The moon was a few days away from being full. The lights from the ship's lanterns reflected off the water.

"Where to begin?" Markus paused. "You may want to take notes. I'll try to explain it as best as I can, but it is like trying to explain what came first, the chicken or the egg. The whole time travel thing is, well, very twisted."

"Which are we, the chicken or the egg?" Trinity asked.

"You, Trinity, are the egg."

Markus sat down before the teens who had grown into adults over the last fifteen years. He looked at each of them. "First, I have to tell you how much I admire your courage and strength. What you did, what you survived is…I don't think any other persons could have done what you did."

Trinity reached out and took Jacob's hand.

"OK, from the beginning. I will lay this out as best as I can. You see, Trinity's message to her parents, to your parents, made it. But not when you thought it would have. It all started back in the sixties, when news of Trinity's message started to leak out. From this news, scientists started to map, record, the solar fields coming from the sun. From your message, Trinity, we had a starting point, or knew where and when the starting point would be."

Markus looked to see if they were following along.

"You see, that day you went into the cave, we were there, watching. We had placed a time capsule a few days before in the same area of the mountain, which time shifted with you. This capsule recorded the magnetic fields in the shift. It recorded the exact time, day, everything. The capsule went back in time with you. And there it sat, recording information, until we or the scientists of the time entered the cave the afternoon you disappeared to once again retrieve it."

"OK, so tell me how it recorded info if any powered device loses all power during time travel. Not like it had a solar cell to charge it in the cave," Jacob said.

"Good point, Jacob. It had a small fusion fuel cell which brought it back online about two days later. Once back online, it recorded the magnetic fields in the cave for the next two hundred and seventy-five years. For the scientists watching it, it was like it never left, but in fact, it had travelled back in time and sat there waiting for two hundred and seventy-five years. On it, it recorded both sides of the gate—the present and the past. What was key, were the magnetic fields on both sides."

Jacob leaned forward with interest as Markus continued to talk.

"At the time, this information was of little use to the science team of the day. But, fast-forward three hundred and twenty-two years, and with this information and the recorded solar activity over the last three hundred fifty years, it all started to make sense. What we learned was how you affect the gate, or field, on one end determines where you get off on the other end.

"In 2337, we were able to use all this information and fold space when the conditions were right. Now what you have to understand is the conditions, or gates, only happen once or twice a year. In some years, they do not happen at all. It's subject to what part of the world, or gate, you are in."

"There are more than the Chungo Cave?" Trinity asked.

"Oh yes." Markus picked up his black bag and pulled out a black object, ten by seventeen inches and one inch thick. The object was void of any reflections. It was as black as a black hole, no light reflecting off of it. Markus opened the object up, and the four students learned that it was some form of laptop computer from the year 2337. A holographic keypad came to life on the lower half of the computer. Markus typed in a password, and the screen came alive.

"OK, that is f-ing cool," Tom said.

"How the hell does that work?" Jacob asked.

"It is a data terminal made from graphene, and the light from the sun charges it from any side. In theory, it will run forever," Markus pointed out.

On the screen appeared sixteen locations on the earth with markers. One was the Chungo Caves in Alberta.

"To answer your question, there are sixteen gates throughout the world that we know of right now; all are subterranean in some way. Subject to the sun, the time of year, any of these gates can be used. But, as I said, in some years, a gate may not work at all."

"So you go to any of these caves and what?" Keara asked.

Markus put up his hand. "Let me finish the rest of the story. In 2337, we more or less understood most of how it worked, the window, or crossing. So we sent a team to the Chungo Cave, and there the team set up a three-point field-generating grid system which we used to trip the gate, or crossing. What we learned was it can take around six or so days for a gate to trip, meaning you have to sit there for as long as six days. A gate can trip anytime in those six days. In some cases, it can happen in a few hours, and in others, it can take five or more days."

"So, what, you sit in this field grid waiting?" Trinity asked.

"Yes. Exactly! What we also found out is it is not an exact target at the other end either. Like the way in, the way out is a window of plus or minus three days. So you do not know the exact day or time you will arrive from the future. In the case of the first science team who went back to 1739, it arrived one day before you did. They could have possibly arrived after you had left the cave or the same time you crossed over."

Markus paused and once again looked at his audience to see if he had lost them.

"The team worked through the night to clear the cave of all the scientific equipment for your arrival from 2014. And then there you were, the seven of you."

Markus moved his hands around the computer screen to reveal a video image of the seven teens leaving the cave.

"Oh my God," Keara said.

The four were left speechless at what they were seeing. They looked at each other not knowing what to make of all this.

"You were there!" Trinity called out.

"I wasn't, but my wife, Jessica, was. She was in charge of the expedition to 1739, to the Chungo Caves," Markus pointed out. "This was the greatest scientific mission of all time."

"You could have stopped us from going in 2014, or the people who watched us in 2014 could have stopped us," Keara said.

"You would think so, but no, Keara."

"They couldn't stop us, for if they did, none of this would have happened. Everything we did, and still will do, would not have happened, and it would go against what was meant to unfold," Jacob said.

Markus looked to Jacob and nodded. "Very profound and correct, Jacob. Everything in this timeline, or perhaps in any timeline, is predestined. We all have our part to play."

"So what happened next with the science team?" Trinity asked.

"Next, having recorded your arrival, the team set up a secret solar observatory on top of the mountain, which was hidden in the rocks. It sat there for five hundred and ninety-eight years until the data from it was collected. With it, we had a road map from 1739 to 2337. We knew when all the gates, or windows, would open and when they could be used. We knew how to adjust the exit point so we could control the end year as best as possible."

Markus looked uneasy now. He looked at the four. He wanted to say more, but was now looking for the right words.

"What you have to understand is since there is a six-day window to cross a gate, you cannot use a gate twice. Meaning, if you leave, say, on March 24, 2014, you cannot return on the same window or gate. This is because of the danger of overlap. There is a high probability, sixty per-cent, that you will return before you leave."

"OK, that's screwed," Tom said.

"What would happen if you did?" Trinity asked.

"Two objects cannot occupy the same space, in this case, two of the same person. We do not fully know, but you would have a paradox, and one or both of the objects would cease to exist in time."

"OK, so how do you return to your future if the map you are fol-lowing doesn't have the next gate listed on it because it doesn't exist yet? Like a future gate, since you cannot use the same gate to return," Trinity said.

"Very good, Trinity, you understand. As time moves forward in the future tense, you finally record or discover the next window coming up. This information is loaded into a pod or probe and sent back to the past date. In some cases, it can arrive before the science team does. It could be waiting for you."

Markus looked at Trinity.

Jacob sat back in his chair. "You're right, I have to write this down. Holy crap, this is twisted!"

"In the case of my wife, Jessica, and her team, the pod showed up a few days after you left the cave. The problem was the next gate for the time period was the following summer in May 1740." Markus tried to crack a smile. "Unlike you, who headed south and then west to the coast to fend off the winter, they stayed. They tried to ride out the winter." He became silent.

"She didn't make it," Trinity said.

Markus looked up. "No, none of them made it. My Jessica and eleven of my best friends froze to death that winter."

Tears formed in Trinity's eyes. "I'm sorry."

Markus fought back the tears. "Nothing to be sorry for, Trinity. However you want to look at it, she has now been dead for the last fifteen or five hundred ninety-seven years." Markus closed the black slate computer.

"Why are you here?" Jacob asked.

"Why indeed. You see, my fellow scientists had what they needed. I…We all knew there was something wrong the second we sent the probe back with the new gate info. They should have returned right after, or even before, we sent the probe, based on the length of the window. But nothing! I fought with them to send a rescue team. After all, they were my friends. She was my wife, and I loved her. Finally I got my way, and we launched a rescue from an island cave in the Andaman Sea, where we had our main lab. There were four of us, and we brought back a VTOL aircraft and flew from the Andaman Sea to Canada and the Chungo Cave. But, it was too late. The universe would not give my Jessica back to me. It would not give me a gate close enough in time to save her. When we arrived, we found them there, huddled together, in a collapsed tent."

Markus moved toward Trinity. "When I look at you, I see her. She was loving, beautiful, caring, a gift in my life. The ground was so frozen that we couldn't bury them. So we piled their bodies and burned them. There is not a day which goes by that I do not think of her. When I read your story, the story you sent through time, I felt your pain not being able to say good-bye to your loved ones."

Trinity looked to her friends.

"After that, we headed west to the Hawaiian Islands, where we landed to refuel the aircraft with new fuel cells. It was then that I did something I cannot change. I took the aircraft and left the three other team members there, stranded in this time."

Keara looked up at Markus.

"If it is any consolation, they were all assholes, and I did leave them in paradise."

"Why?" Keara asked.

"Why indeed. Because in grief, we do things which we regret later. I took the aircraft, the field gate generators, and the gate key and headed east, finally making it to the East Coast of North America. I destroyed the aircraft and pushed it into the sea. There, like you, I started a new life. Or I tried to. Unlike you, I had the history of the world at my fingertips. Everything which was to happen from 1739 on was documented. With the gate key and gate generators, I started to move around time, always looking for something, that something that would replace my love for my wife. I tried different ways to go back in time before she froze to death. But, I never found it."

Markus made his way over to a table with a number of drink bottles.

"May I?" Markus pointed to the bottles.

Trinity nodded in approval. Markus poured a glass of rum.

"Why are you here?" Trinity asked again.

"Two reasons, the first to warn you. Because of my actions, my fellow Gatekeepers have been looking for me for the last five hundred and thirty-seven years, to stop me from passing through any more gates. They believe everything has a place in time, and a reason, and by doing what I was doing, I would change that. The fact I am here telling what I know goes against what is to happen."

"The second?" Trinity asked.

"Because of love, and to give you peace of mind. To tell you your parents went to sleep knowing all ended as it should. They knew what became of you. And that you were always faithful to the end when it came to your love for them. To give you peace in knowing that."

Trinity started to cry. She could no longer hold back the tears. Keara made her way over to comfort her, hold her.

Markus lifted his glass to Trinity. He held it high. "I lift my glass to you, Trinity. I lift my glass to all of you. You all have a special bond. Hold on to it. And know in the end your parents loved you as much as you loved them." Markus took a drink. "It is late; I think I have filled your minds with quite a lot of information for one night. I am very tired now, and when I get tired, I start having to deal with my demons."

Markus put his glass down. "Good night. Always be faithful to the end."

"Good night, Mr. Keel," Trinity said, wiping the tears from her eyes.

And with that, Markus Keel picked up his slate computer, placed it in the black bag, and opened the door and left for his room.

Trinity, Jacob, Keara, and Tom were left in the room speechless. They looked at each other. It was like a giant stone had been lifted from them. A man from the future had come and, in a single night, answered all their questions.

From outside the door, Bianca peeked in. "Mamá?"

Trinity wiped the last of the tears from her eyes. "Yes, Bianca, what can we do for you?"

"It's late."

"I know, dear. Your father and I will see you to bed."

Trinity smiled at her, and then she and Jacob, followed by Tom and Keara, started to leave the room.

"You're welcome to stay the night; your room is always ready," Trinity said.

"I think we will take you up on that offer," Tom said.

As they left, Jacob blew out the last of the oil lamps.

As Jacob and I walked to put Bianca and Christopher to bed, I kept thinking about what Markus had said. I felt sad for Markus losing his wife as he did. I thought about what it must have been like finding her in the snow, frozen, lifeless. I thought about how amazing the technology was that allowed him and others to cross time and space. And finally, I thought back to my wish that whatever happened, my parents should not stop us from leaving on that day for the cave. It was clear they could have stopped us. But they didn't, and for that I was grateful. Life was hard, but all these years later, my only regret was not saying good-bye. Other than that, I was happy, and my children were happy. What more could one want?

Chapter Three

Knowing

August 22, 1754

The sound of the ocean could be heard outside the dining room windows as Trinity, Jacob, Keara, and Tom met for breakfast at 8:43a.m. The four sat around the table waiting, each looking at the empty chair that was reserved for Markus. Their eyes drifted around to each other and then back to the chair. Jacob pulled out his pocket watch and looked at the time.

"How did you sleep?" Trinity asked Keara and Tom.

"How do you think?" Keara replied.

"Yes…a few things to relive and think about."

"I guess Markus had no problem sleeping," Jacob said.

"Seriously, I can't wait anymore. He manages to cross five-hundred-some years and then can't wake up on time for breakfast. Give me a break," Trinity said as she stood to leave the dining room.

"Where you going?" Keara asked.

"To see what is taking our guest so long."

Trinity started to leave as Jacob stood to follow her.

Trinity, Jacob, Keara, and Tom arrived at the door to Markus's guest room. Trinity knocked, and the four stood there waiting. Trinity looked to Jacob, who then moved up to the door and knocked even louder. Nothing. Jacob tried the door, and it opened.

"What the hell, did he leave in the night?" Keara asked.

Jacob swung the door open, and they entered the room. The window was open, and the drapes danced softly in the morning breeze. As they looked around, Trinity was the first to see Markus on the bed. He was stretched out, lying on top of the sheets, still dressed from the night before. Slowly, Trinity and the others moved toward him. As they got closer, it was clear by his color he was dead.

"Oh my God!" Trinity said.

Jacob and Tom moved past Trinity to get a closer look. There was no question Markus Keel had passed away. Next to him, on a small night table, was a note and an open bottle of pills. Jacob looked down at the body and then over at the pills and note. He picked up the note and then handed it to Trinity.

Trinity read out loud. "'It was a great honor to meet you all in person; it fulfilled many years of my life, and by doing so, I brought my journey here to an end. I now join my Jessica and your friends Kim, Andy, and Robert. Love is a powerful thing. Always faithful. Cum dilectione. With love. Markus Keel.'"

Trinity dropped the note to her side. She just looked at Markus, almost with disappointment in her eyes. Keara and Tom moved in to get a better look at Markus lying there.

"He killed himself," Keara said. "What kind of man kills himself?"

"A sad man who has no one or nowhere to go to anymore," Trinity said.

August 23, 1754

In a fenced-in graveyard, Trinity, Jacob, Keara, and Tom were joined by their four children, Bianca, Christopher, Erich, and Josh. They stood there and said their good-byes to Markus Keel as his body was lowered into an open grave. A young friar waved the last rites over the body and spoke in Spanish a few last words. They were joined by a number of the house staff who looked on.

The late-afternoon sun cast its long shadows across the grave site. The summer grass swayed in the gentle breeze. Behind them was the entrance to their shared family tomb. The friar finished and then dropped some soil into the grave. Trinity followed, as did the others, who repeated the same gesture.

"Good-bye, Markus. I hope you found what you were looking for," Trinity said.

That night, the four friends found themselves once again in the guest room that had held Markus. Trinity stood looking out the window at Markus's ship still at anchor. She then turned and saw Markus's black bag. She picked it up and pulled from it the black slate computer and placed it on the bed. Trinity slowly ran her fingers across the cover of the unit.

Keara looked to Trinity and the computer. She knew what Trinity was thinking. She then turned to Tom.

"I think it is time we go home. Good night, Jacob. Good night, Trinity," Keara said. She turned to leave, and Tom joined her.

Trinity looked down at the slate computer.

Jacob looked toward her as he walked to the door. "Tomorrow, Trinity, not tonight."

August 24, 1754

The day began with Trinity on the balcony with the slate computer. She had it open and was trying to log in. But every time she tried, the unit would kick her out or, after a time, just shut down. Jacob walked up behind her and looked down at her failure.

"Don't you have work in the fields with the staff, bananas to bring in?" Trinity asked.

"You don't think you're going to actually get into that thing."

"One can try."

"Then what?"

"I don't know. One thing at a time."

Jacob leaned over to Trinity and kissed her. "Have a good day. Bye."

Trinity tried a few more times and then closed the cover and set the computer to the side. She stood and then walked over to the stone railing wall and looked down to the sea. As she looked down, she saw that there were four rowboats on the shore now. The crew of Markus's ship had left it, and it was now at anchor, with no one aboard.

Trinity turned and ran after Jacob, trying to stop him. "Jacob!" She ran down the stairs to the main hall. As she arrived in the courtyard, she was just able to stop Jacob from riding off for the day.

"What is it, Trinity?" he said.

"I think the crew of Markus's ship has left it, and I think there's no one aboard. If that's the case, we have to go have a look."

Jacob looked down at her from atop his horse. "Agreed." Jacob called to Felipe to get Trinity's horse and to find a few men to help row one of the small boats.

An hour later, Trinity and Jacob, with the aid of Felipe and three field hands, pushed one of the four rowboats into the sea and started rowing toward the twin-masted sailing ship that had brought Markus to the shores of La Palma island.

Fifteen minutes had passed and Trinity and Jacob climbed aboard the ship with Felipe in tow. As Trinity had guessed, the ship was deserted. The crew had left the ship adrift, with only the anchor line to provide any protection for it.

Trinity and Jacob stood there. "Weird. Why leave?" Trinity asked.

"Perhaps they knew that Markus would not be coming back," Jacob responded. "Let's look around."

The three started to search the sailing ship. As they made their way below deck, it was clear the crew had cleared the ship out, taking whatever they could carry. Everything was stripped bare.

"This way," Jacob said to Trinity as he pointed down the hall to the back of the ship. "If Markus was captain, his cabin should be back here."

The three made their way to the stern of the ship and the captain's cabin. As Jacob pushed the door open, they saw it was more or less cleaned out. They walked through the cabin and saw a number of maps and charts stretched out on the main desk.

Jacob looked at the maps. "Looks like Markus has been everywhere in the last few years."

Trinity walked past Jacob, looking at a number of framed drawings on the cabin walls. One caught her attention; it was of a man and African woman. Trinity looked closer at it.

"Jacob, come here. This is Andy, isn't it, but older."

Jacob walked over to Trinity and looked at the sketch. "It is. Who is the woman next to him?"

Trinity smiled. Just then, something caught her eye under the captain's bunk. Jacob looked to Trinity and then toward the bunk. Just sticking out from it was a silver-grey round tube end, about four inches in diameter. Jacob moved down to his knees and pulled out a round three-foot-long tube. He then looked and found two more and pulled them out.

Jacob turned to Felipe and spoke to him in Spanish, asking him to go back up on deck and see if he could find a bag to take the tubes off the ship. Felipe nodded and turned to leave.

After Felipe left, Jacob started to turn the lid on one of the tubes and began to unscrew it. He then turned it over, and Trinity watched as a futuristic-looking device slid out. It was dark blue in color and had yellow markings all over it, with red-and-black cooling fins halfway up toward the top. On the top, there looked to be solar cells to charge it after use.

"What are they?" Trinity asked.

"Markus's field generators," Jacob responded.

"No…"

"Yeah." Jacob smiled.

They heard Felipe coming down the hall. Jacob slid the unit back into the tube and closed it. Felipe entered with a tan bag and handed it to Jacob, who stuffed in the three tubes. Trinity pulled the sketch of Andy and the African woman from the wall.

"What now?" Trinity asked.

"I will take Felipe in the morning, and we will ride into Santa Cruz and look for a small crew to sail the ship back to port there," Jacob said.

"That will take you two days round trip."

"Yes, I know, but we can't leave the ship here."

Ten minutes later, Trinity and Jacob, with the field hands, pushed off from the ship with their tan bag in tow. As the workers rowed, Trinity looked back at the ship. It reminded her of all the times she had been at sea. How she hated it at times. She then turned and looked at her home high in the hills overlooking the sea below. How she loved the home Jacob and she had built.

August 25, 1754

Trinity, Keara, and Tom sat in the tower fortress atop the estate home. Situated around the room were the three field generators, and center stage was the graphene slate computer. Once again, Trinity was trying to break the password set by Markus.

"What have you tried?" Keara asked.

"What haven't I tried?" Trinity replied.

Tom was handling one of the field, or gate, generators. "Over the years I have forgotten what quality workmanship looks like. These are so cool. Any clue how they work?" he asked Trinity.

"No, Jacob thinks the top black area is the solar cells to charge them after the fold in time."

"I can't see the point of getting into his computer," Keara said.

"Why, don't you want to know?"

"Know what, the future? The next five hundred years?"

"Yes."

"Trinity, some things are better left alone. You cling to dreams of saying good-bye, and we know you did. We…You know your message made it." Keara turned toward the desk and looked at the manuscript bound by string, which consisted of the first 1,212 days of their journey from Nordegg, Alberta, which ended on La Palma in 1742. She stepped forward and picked up the drawing of Andy and the African woman by his side. She looked at it. "I wonder if this was in Cuba? And if so, I hope he is happy. Do we know who the woman is?"

Trinity sat there quietly, not saying anything.

"Good night, Trinity. Send our best to Jacob once he returns from Santa Cruz," Tom said. He moved over to Trinity, sitting on the chair, and gave her a hug and kiss. "Adiós, see you in the next few days. Good luck with your project."

Keara and Tom departed.

Later that night, Trinity sat watching the sunset, which she tried to do as often as possible. Tonight the sunset was especially beautiful. As Trinity sat there, Bianca joined her mother on the balcony.

"Como estás?" Bianca asked.

"Bianca, dear, come join me."

Bianca sat down next to her mother, and the two of them sat looking at the fire setting into the sea.

"What's wrong, Mamá?" Bianca said.

Trinity looked at her daughter and smiled. "Does it show?"

"It does."

"Sorry, dear, I must learn to be more happy."

"Mamá?"

"Yes, Bianca?"

"Christopher and I were talking. Why is it that we, me and Christopher, have no grandparents? Erich and Josh also do not have any grandparents. Everyone else we know has *abuelos*, but not us. Did they die before we were born? Why, in all these years, have you never once talked about them?"

Trinity looked at her and was at a loss for words.

"Did they make you angry? Is that why you never talk about them?"

Trinity continued to look at her. Tears were forming in her eyes. "No, dear, they never made me angry. On the contrary, they made me proud." She wiped the tears from her eyes as she looked for the right words to say. "Come here, dear, so I can hold you."

Bianca sat next to her mother as Trinity hugged her daughter tight.

"Someday I will find the courage to tell you all about them and how special they were…and how special you and your brother are."

August 26, 1754

Christopher ran out to meet his father as he rode in with Felipe and two small wagons filled with sailors to crew Markus's ship. Jacob jumped down and gave him a hug. A few minutes later, Bianca ran out to join them.

"Where's your mother?" Jacob asked Bianca.

"I don't know."

"Well, good to see you again," Jacob said.

From a window on the top floor of the estate, Trinity looked down at Jacob and her children below. She stood there with her arms crossed, a look of mixed emotions on her face.

Later that night, Trinity and Jacob sat for dinner joined by Bianca and Christopher.

"How was your trip?" Trinity asked.

"Good, good, we have enough crew to sail the ship to Santa Cruz."

"What then?" Trinity asked.

"Sorry? What do you mean?"

"What are you going to do with the ship?"

"I don't know, sell it? Not like we have any need for a ship. When we go to Lisbon, we book passage with Captain Guzman. You know that."

Trinity just sat there and ate her food. Jacob looked over to Bianca and Christopher.

"Bianca, Christopher, can you excuse us? I would like a word with your mother."

The two children looked at each other. They took a few more bites of food, then slid their chairs out and ran out of the room laughing.

Trinity looked up. "They weren't finished."

"Yes, nor are you."

"Sorry?" Trinity said.

"Markus's visit has destroyed the peace we have known here for the last twelve or so years. Ever since he stepped into this house, you have not been the same. He opened all those old wounds again, the pain you have felt for never saying good-bye."

Trinity pushed her plate away and walked out of the room.

"Trinity, I'm sorry!" Jacob called after her. He sat there and then threw his napkin toward the centre of the table.

Cristina walked in to see what was going on. "Señor, hay algo que pueda hacer?"

"Sí, Cristina, mas vino por favor," Jacob said as he lifted his glass of wine.

Later that night, Jacob joined Trinity in their bedroom. The only light was from a few candles that burned around the room. The moon was full, and the ocean breeze blew in softly. It felt good.

Jacob sat down next to Trinity in bed as she continued to work on Markus's black slate computer. "You know, I'm not the enemy here. Last time I looked, I was your friend," he said.

"You are my friend."

"Good, at least we agree on that." Jacob looked down at the computer. "What passwords have you used?"

"You know, I don't know anymore. I've tried everything, even my own name."

"Yeah, he liked you so much he used your name as a password. Keep dreaming, dear."

"He wouldn't have left it if he didn't want me to figure it out. He sailed around the world to find us and tell his story, just to kill himself? I think he wanted more for us."

"Maybe so, but he should have left us the password."

Trinity looked to Jacob. "Where is his last message, his good-bye note?"

"I don't know."

Trinity got out of bed and looked on her desk for Markus's last words. She moved through the pile of paper. Then she found it. She moved closer to the candle to read it.

"God, I can't see any more in the dark!" Over and over again she read it. "Give me the laptop," Trinity said to Jacob.

"Please."

"Please give me the laptop."

Jacob took the computer and handed to Trinity. She took it and sat down at her desk, then started to type.

"What is it?"

"Quiet!" Trinity typed and then typed again. "Shit."

"What?"

"His last line includes 'Always faithful.' Does that not sound out of place? And he would always say that from time to time when he talked. I remember him saying it over and over again."

"Come to bed, Trinity. It's late, and I have to get an early start tomorrow. We still have a harvest to get in, and I have to meet Oscar to review the next set of diamonds we will sell in Lisbon next month," Jacob said.

Trinity sat at the desk. "Jacob, do you remember the licence plate my dad had on his black Suburban?"

"What? You're kidding. Trinity, that was fifteen years ago. I can't remember what I had."

"His front one, the red-and-gold one."

"Yes, it was a Marine Corps logo."

"Yes, right. What was the saying?"

Jacob sat up in the bed and looked at Trinity.

"What was it?" she called out.

"I'm thinking!"

"Semper…something."

"Semper Fi," Jacob said. "Look at the note in the bottom corner, the words 'cum dilectione,' which is 'with love' in Latin."

Trinity typed in "semper fi." But nothing. Then she tried it again as "Semper Fi," and this time the slate computer came to life.

"Oh my God! That's it. That's it!"

Jacob stepped from the bed, made his way over to Trinity, and stood looking over her shoulder. "Well, way to go, dear, way to go."

Trinity turned and looked back to Jacob with a smile. She kissed him and gave him a hug.

"We're not sleeping tonight, are we?"

"Ah, no," Trinity said as she moved her fingers over the hologram mouse pad.

August 27, 1754

Morning came, and Trinity was still at work on the computer. Jacob was asleep on the bed. Then there was the morning knock on the door, which could only mean the start of the morning ritual.

"Un minuto." Trinity closed the lid on the computer and slid it into the desk. "Pase."

The door swung open, and Cristina stepped in with her tray.

Slowly Jacob started to come to life, one eye and then the other.

"Good morning," Trinity said.

"Hi" was the soft reply from Jacob. "You figured it out?"

"Yes, very close. Almost everything is here about history, how the gates work, where the gates are, and the dates you can cross over between them. But, I need your help with a lot of this."

"All right. I will send Felipe to the fields today without me. But first, let's have breakfast."

After breakfast, Jacob and Trinity returned to their tower hideout. Jacob opened the computer and logged in. He was having a hard time with it. Fifteen years without the use of a computer had robbed him of his quick skills. Jacob spent the next hour trying to go through the system.

"This is interesting," he said as he gazed up, looking for Trinity, who was now fast asleep on the couch. Jacob closed the lid to the machine, made his way next to Trinity, and lay down, trying to find some room for himself. He hugged her and then fell asleep.

That night, Keara and Tom joined Trinity and Jacob for dinner.

"You know, we've spent more time with you this last month than we have in the last year," Keara said.

"I know. Nice, isn't it?" Jacob said.

"How's your project coming?" Tom asked.

"I'm in!" Trinity smiled.

Keara and Tom looked at Trinity in disbelief. They turned to Jacob for confirmation.

Jacob nodded his head. "Yes, she is in."

"No shit!" Keara said. "Well?"

"There is a lot to talk about," Trinity said.

"I bet there is. How is it you always manage to wreck dinner at the start for us?" Keara looked over to Cristina and the other staff members and then continued to talk in a soft whisper. "Now I need to know what's on the computer."

Trinity took a bite of her food and smiled at Tom and Keara with a look of "if you only knew." Jacob took a drink of his wine and lifted it toward Trinity, congratulating her for a job well done.

As the last candle was put out, the four left the dining room and walked through the house, toward the stairs that would take them to the tower. But as they did, they passed the study and saw Bianca, Christopher, Erich, and Josh sitting together around the fireplace as it burned. Trinity stopped and looked at the children. She smiled.

"Were we ever that young?" Trinity asked.

Keara, too, stopped and looked at her own children. "Yes, I think so. But that was a long time ago, in a time which no longer exists."

"Someday it will again, when we are long gone," Trinity said.

In the tower room, the four sat looking at the slate computer and three field gate generators.

"We could go home," Trinity said.

Keara looked over to Trinity. "We are home; this is the home we built for ourselves. This is the home Robert, Kim, and Andy died for."

"I know. I just want to see them one more time. I want my children to know who their grandparents were, and who they are."

"Markus was clear that we cannot travel without affecting the future," Jacob said.

"We wouldn't affect the future. I just want to see them from afar. I want Bianca to see them, and I want Christopher to know who they were. I want to set eyes on them before I die."

"Then what?" Tom asked.

"Then we come home, and I go on with my life, live life as it was meant to be lived. I go to sleep finally being at peace. I watch our children grow up and move on with their lives knowing they are special, knowing their parents were special."

Tom and Keara looked at each other. "I try to forget about my parents, friends, loved ones. I was getting good at it. Then you bring this all up again," Keara said.

Tom smiled. "What is to say it was not meant to happen? After all, if you choose to believe everything is pre-set, then how can we not but try?"

"If we do this, and I mean *if*, how do you plan to make it happen? There is no way we can go back to the Chungo Cave. That's impossible. It was just dumb luck we made it in the first place," Keara said.

"Jacob has a plan," Trinity said.

"Well, let's hear it, smartass," Keara said.

Jacob made his way over to the desk and pulled out a world map. He laid the map on the table in front of them and pointed. "No, the cave we came through is out. Too old to even think we could make that trip again. There is a gate right here in our backyard, or so to speak. According to the locations, we could use a set of caves right here on the island, about thirty kilometres from here. They would work."

Trinity looked on with excitement. "Before you get too excited, the set of caves only has a window every few years. Next one is 1756, which we could wait for. But, if we are to make this happen sooner, we would have to use a gate in Chile. It looks like the farther you go north or south toward the poles, the more active the gates are and the closer the time periods are to using them. If we use Chile, we would have to sail to Argentina and overland from there to southern Chile, an area called Patagonia. Once there, find and enter the cave, wait, and jump or step through the gate to 2015 or 2016. There are countless end dates we can use, right up to 2337."

"And then what? My parents aren't in Chile, nor are yours. How do we get out of Chile to Canada? I left my passport at home fifteen years ago and have not been back to get it," Keara joked.

"Yes, that was a problem of living in a Big Brother world. However, Trinity has family there, and they may be able to help. Regardless, once in Chile, we make our way to the German and British embassies. There, Trinity, who is also a German citizen, uses her fingerprint to back up her nationality. Keara does the same with the UK passport, but for her, it would be something they call a Biometric scan. The hope is that Trinity and Keara get back into the system. Once in, we come up with some BS story why you and I and the kids don't have passports, like we have lived in Chile for the last twenty years and now need passports to travel outside."

"Sorry, that plan sounds like bullshit," Keara said.

"Yeah, well, with luck, they issue, and then we add the children too. If not, we are stuck in Chile, waving bye to you girls leaving for Canada."

"Have to agree with Keara, big if. In 1970, yes; in 2016, not going to happen. How many diamonds are we going to take to buy what we need?" Tom asked.

"A few. We may need to buy passports when it's all said and done," Jacob said.

Tom stood and walked over to one of the field gate generators. Picking it up, he turned to Trinity. "When the time comes, it means six or more weeks at sea, if we follow Jacob again."

"I know, but when the time comes, I hope we can use the gate in our backyard."

"Still need passports to get off the island in 2016," Jacob said.

"But Europe is just across the sea," Trinity pointed out.

"Keara, your thoughts?" Tom asked.

Keara looked at Tom, then to Trinity. "I love you like a sister, always have. I have followed you to the ends of the earth." There is a long pause. "When we are ready, I will do this one more time, for our children."

"Thank you!" Trinity said.

"Nothing to thank. We all need this."

"When do you see all this happening?" Tom asked.

"I know Trinity would like to go tomorrow, but I think we should give it a few years, let the children get older. We have to start preparing them slowly. I can only guess what kind of shock this would be on them."

"Yes, I still remember how shocking it was for us," Keara said. She looked down at her hand and arm; at the scar from the bear attack she suffered. She moved her fingers. "Yes, they will need time to understand who they are."

Later that night, as the last of the lights were dimmed, Trinity lay beside Jacob in their bed. She looked out the open window at the stars up high; the moon was just over the horizon, a giant yellowy-orange ball moving its way into the night sky.

Jacob put his arms around her and held her tight.

"Thank you," Trinity said to Jacob.

"I, too, want the chance to say good-bye."

With that, Jacob kissed Trinity.

Chapter Four

Semper Fi

September 15, 1754

Jacob sat at the desk in the tower room, reviewing the information on the slate computer. As he read, he made notes on parchment. There was something that caught his eye. He moved his hand around, waving it, moving the files and information from one screen to the next. As he did, his look became more intense. He ran his hands through his long hair.

He finally picked up his glasses, put them on, and sat back in his chair, looking at the room around him. He stood and walked out onto the open balcony. There he gazed out at the sea and the home below him. Looking to the sky, he saw a number of seagulls circling. He studied them for the longest time. Finally he pulled his pocket watch out, opened it, and looked at the time. He stared at it, thinking back to the day Trinity gave it to him in 1742 in Lisbon. The time was 5:55. Finally closing it, he retreated back into the tower.

September 18, 1754

The group of four met in the study to talk about the plan to time travel to 2016. Tom closed the large double doors so the four would not be disturbed. He then sat down next to Keara across from Trinity and Jacob.

"So why the rush, Jacob? Why talk about this again? You said the children should be older, and Keara and I agree," Tom said.

Jacob looked at Trinity.

"What, Jacob? You're the one who is now suggesting going sooner rather than later. I agree with Keara. We can go whenever, I mean, subject to the dates that line up with the gates in Chile or in our backyard. After all, time is on our side now," Trinity said.

Jacob looked at the group before him for the longest time. He then pulled out a number of sheets of parchment that contained the notes he had compiled over the last few weeks. He lifted his glasses so he could read them. As he did, he looked up at the now-finished family portrait of Trinity, himself and the children hanging over the fireplace. He smiled.

"That's the thing. Time is not really on our side, not anymore."

"Sorry?" Tom said.

Jacob looked to Trinity. "Our journey is coming to an end." He turned to Trinity "Trinity, on December 21, 1757, you will die."

Trinity was shocked!

"If it gives you any comfort, I'll join you on January 11, 1758."

Keara and Tom looked at each other not knowing what to say.

"No, don't say it," Keara said. She turned back to Tom.

Tom looked at Jacob. "When do we…?"

"Goddamn it, Tom. Do not do this." Keara turned to Jacob. "How dare you. Some things are better left alone."

"It's too late, Keara," Tom said. "He knows, and how do you think we can go through life, , knowing that Jacob knows? We could never look at him again the same way, always thinking in the back of our minds he knows. He knows."

Keara stood and paced around the room. As she did, she looked at Trinity with contempt in her eyes. This was the first time Keara ever had this look toward her best friend.

"Damn it, Trinity, damn it, Markus, I hate you for coming here." Keara finally stopped pacing and looked at Tom. "How long do we have?"

Jacob looked to Tom. Tom nodded.

"Keara, you will pass away on May 2, 1760."

Keara stopped, tilted her head back, and looked at the ceiling.

Jacob continued. "Tom, you're the lucky one. You live to April 12, 1780."

Tom looked to Keara. He was about to say something, but then stopped.

Keara looked down at him. "I guess you do OK without me."

Tom looked at Trinity and finally at Jacob. "Is the information good? I mean, is it accurate?" he asked.

"I would think so. After all, to the Gatekeepers, we are the reason for everything. How our lives ended would be of great importance to them."

"Well," Trinity said, looking around the room, "I don't know if I should be thankful or sad."

"It's like knowing you have a fatal disease and you only have six weeks to live," Keara said.

Trinity walked over to her painting. "I guess we should…I guess I should make the best of the last three years of my life." She looked back at her friends. "I know what I have to do."

Jacob looked to Keara and Tom.

Tom then spoke. "When do we leave?"

All eyes were now on Jacob.

"Well, you started this," Tom pointed out.

Jacob pulled his notes out and lifted his glasses to read them. "The next usable gate in Chile is in three months. This is the closest we can get in the time that is left for the two of us. Subject to how long we stay, and where we plan our return, we could be back in this time in summer 1755. The children go on with their lives, and we…and we wait for the end."

"That should give us enough time to put things in order before… we join our friends," Trinity said.

Later that night, Trinity sat before her piano and slowly played. The sound was soothing to Jacob, who stood nearby on the balcony, looking out at the setting sun. Trinity finally ended her song and looked down at the keys, thinking. She wanted to play more, but couldn't make herself. Finally she pushed the bench back and hit a few more keys out of order, then made her way to Jacob.

Trinity's long brown hair blew in the wind. She brushed it from her face and turned to Jacob. "Do you think there are sunsets in heaven?"

Jacob looked back to her. "Yes, Trinity, more beautiful than these ever were. And music all the time to put a smile on your face."

"Good." Trinity hugged Jacob and held him tight. She started to cry.

"I love you," Jacob said.

"I know. I know."

Chapter Five

Westbound

November 3, 1754

The sun was high in the sky, not a cloud in sight, and Santa Cruz, was alive with people as Trinity, Jacob, Keara, Tom, and their four children rode into the port. Trinity jumped down from the carriage, then turned to help Bianca and Christopher down. Jacob jumped down from his horse and stood next to his family. They were then joined by Keara, Tom, Erich, and Josh.

Trinity walked down to the berth. There, tied up, was Markus's old ship. She stopped and looked at the stern. There, in gold and blue letters across the back, was the name *Semper Fi*. Trinity turned and looked back at Jacob. She smiled.

"No way," Trinity said.

"Always faithful, dear," Jacob said.

"You know, when you are given a finite time, you see the world very differently. You suddenly want to make the most of each day."

Keara walked past Trinity. "Then let us get started."

The two families started to board the ship as the dock workers off-loaded all their belongings and moved them aboard. The ship was in no way large—she was 100 feet—but then again, it was their private ship. Two families and a crew of twenty-five. The *Semper Fi* was commanded by Captain Correa, a man in his late fifties, with brown eyes and long grey hair tied into a ponytail. He was a tired-looking man. If not for Jacob's money, he would be content sitting at home in his later years.

"Señora es un placer tenerla a bordo," Captain Correa said to Trinity.

"Gracias, Capitán. Espero que sea una aventura," Trinity said. She smiled. One more ship, one more journey until she and Jacob would finally leave this world for the greatest journey of all.

The families made their way below deck to their cabins. The ship was alive with crew working to get things ready for sea. The cabins set aside for the two families were small, but there would only be two persons per cabin, so more than enough room for the sixty-day crossing to Argentina.

The children started to settle in and fight over who was going to get which berth. "Enough!" yelled Trinity.

As they stood in the hall, looking at the cabins, the dock workers carried their belongings past them. In a large wooden trunk was the slate computer and field gate generators, their keys to the future.

Jacob spotted the trunk and pointed for the dock worker to put it into the main port-side cabin where Trinity and he would be staying for the next two months. "Gracias," he said to the dockhand.

The four children started to run down the narrow hall, past their parents.

"Slow down!" Keara yelled. "Their first time on a ship and at sea. Hard to believe they had never left La Palma."

"Second time for Erich and Bianca. They were one and one and a half the first time," Trinity said as she looked at the children.

"You OK?" Keara asked Trinity.

"Yes, just trying to figure out how to tell my children what's about to happen."

"Good luck with that, and when you figure it out, let me know. Promise?"

"Sure."

Trinity came up behind Jacob, now in the cabin, putting the trunk away in a safe place. "Never had much luck with these long sea voyages. If someone wasn't trying to sink us, Mother Nature would send a storm our way."

"Well, with luck, none of that happens this time." Jacob leaned forward and kissed Trinity. Trinity held him.

Just then, Bianca and Christopher looked in on their mom and dad.

"Mamá, please?" Bianca said.

"Not now. Give us a minute, please." Trinity said as she closed the door on them.

That night, the *Semper Fi* departed Santa Cruz for the open sea. Its sails were full and the wind to her back. In just over seven weeks' time, the two families would step foot on the shores of Argentina. From there they would make their way to southern Chile and to an uncertain future.

Standing there on the upper boat deck, the eight stood looking back at La Palma island as it slowly faded from view. Bianca and Christopher looked lost. This was the first time they could remember leaving their home.

"Mamá?" Bianca said.

"Yes, dear?"

"Will we ever come home again?"

"Bianca, that I can promise you with all my life. You will be coming home again to these shores."

Trinity held her children close to her side, cherishing every day forward.

December 5, 1754

The cool water of the central Atlantic started to turn warm as the *Semper Fi*, her crew, and passengers sailed south to Argentina. Summer had arrived for the Southern Hemisphere. The days were longer, and Trinity was now getting closer to her goal, her purpose in these last few years.

This morning, Trinity sat on deck, reading a book. The wind was blowing, and the sails were full. As was custom for Trinity, when no one was looking, she would pull out her iPhone and take one more photo. By the grace of God, the phone somehow still worked. But, each photo she now took meant she would have to erase one. The phone was full of photos from years ago, and now she would spend hours flipping through the pictures, trying to decide which, if any, could be lost for all time.

Soon Christmas would be here, and like every year for the last fifteen years, they would spend it as a family. Trinity looked forward to this day. As she sat there, Erich walked up to her.

"Tía Trinity," Erich said.

Trinity looked up from her book. "Sí, Erich, what can I do for you?"

"Where are we going? My mother will not tell us. She just keeps talking around in circles, stuff I do not understand, of far away lands and places that will amaze us," Erich said.

Trinity looked at him. "Yes, that would be your mother."

His big brown eyes were filled with questions and wonder. In the coming days, all this boy knew would be changed forever. Like Trinity and her friends fifteen years ago, he and the other children were about to cross the Rubicon. There would be no turning back. Once across, the small universe they knew would become an infinite place of wonder and magic unlike any they could ever imagine.

"Erich, sit down here for a minute." Trinity pointed to the box next to her.

Erich plopped himself down. Trinity looked at him. Then she opened her hands and pulled out the small iPhone case and showed it to him. Erich's eyes went wide; he had never seen anything like this.

"You see, Erich, the place your mother is taking you to is a magic world that makes things like this."

"Can I touch it?"

"Yes, but you have to very careful with it. It is older than you are, and it carries all my dreams and wishes inside it."

"How can it carry these things?"

"What I am about to show you is for only us right now. In the coming weeks, the others will know, but you have to promise not to tell anyone," Trinity said.

"I promise," Erich said.

"Good, I believe you, for you are a good boy." Trinity turned on the phone and started to show Erich the photos. His eyes widened, and his jaw dropped. He was left speechless. Trinity looked up at him and could see the look of shock on his face. She smiled. "Are you all right?"

"Sí, yes, this is magic!"

As Erich watched Trinity move the photos past him, Keara made her way onto the deck. She looked out to sea and then saw Trinity and Erich together. Then she saw the phone in her hand. Keara stopped and turned to make sure none of the crew were around looking at her and the gift from the future. She walked up to Trinity and Erich. Trinity looked up, followed by Erich.

"Mother!" Erich said.

"I know, Erich. I know. Where we are going, you will see even more of these things."

"I can hardly wait!"

"I know. Very soon now, Erich. In the new year."

Erich looked at the two women and smiled. Trinity quickly covered the case as a crew member made his way on deck toward them. As he walked by, he lifted his hat. The three smiled back at him.

December 18, 1754

Puerto San Julián, Argentina. The *Semper Fi* sailed in at first light, which was around noon this day; the days would be long, lasting sixteen hours before it would be dark again, well after midnight. The morning air was cool, setting the stage for the coming days. The eight stood looking at the small seaport first established in 1520. Puerto San Julián would be their gateway to Patagonia, which was named after the first natives in this region, whom the Spanish called giants. Hence, "Patagonia" meant "Bigfoot."

The ship sailed up the inlet to the small town harbour. On each side of the ship, they could see the bare coastline. It was void of any trees and plant life. Ahead was a group of small buildings that made up the port and town. Everything was sand and grey colored. The only animal life were hundreds of sheep that ran along the coastline as the ship moved southwest. The town consisted of around two hundred Spanish settlers who fought each day for a meager existence.

Bianca and the other children just stood there in disbelief. They had come from an estate home next to the sea, to a barren, treeless land. They looked at each other not knowing what to say or if they should even speak.

"Oh my God. It is like coming to the moon," Trinity said. She turned to Jacob. "Did you know it would be like this?"

"No, no clue," Jacob said.

"It's cold. It's summer, yet cold. I'm not used to this," Trinity noted.

"How far from here do we have to ride to get to the caves?" Keara asked.

Jacob pulled a small map from his pocket and began to unfold it. He looked at it, then lifted his glasses.

"Damn, I wish I could see better close up. As best as I can guess based on maps of the area, six hundred and fifty kilometres by horse and wagon," Jacob said.

Tom looked down at Jacob's map. "You're kidding, right? You're going to find a cave based on that map?"

"Yes, with the info on the computer and our compass, we should have no problem finding the lake. Once on the lake, we can find the caves. That is, if the water is low this year," Jacob pointed out.

Trinity's heart dropped. "It's like being back at the Orange River in Africa."

"Didn't you once say, it was the best of times, it was the worst of times?" Keara said.

Trinity turned, pulling the hair away from her face. "It was. And here we are."

"Here we are," Keara finished.

Slowly the ship started to turn into the port and a small wooden dock that stretched into the sea at the north end of the town. It was low tide, and the ship was going to have problems docking. But, Captain Correa would manage. The *Semper Fi* finally docked just after lunch on December eighteen.

Jacob and Tom went ashore with a few of the crew to make arrangements to find wagons and horses to take them northwest into the Patagonia region.

Trinity and Keara watched as their men departed the ship. Standing next to Trinity was Erich. She turned to him. "Is our secret still safe?" she asked.

"Sí," Erich replied. "Yes."

Late that evening, Jacob and Tom returned. They looked tired after a long day of trying to arrange things. They climbed aboard the ship with the other crew members in tow. Trinity was there to meet him as he stepped onto the deck.

"Well, how did it go?" she asked.

"Good. We have three wagons, a dozen horses, and a boat. With money to spare," Jacob said.

"When do we leave?" Trinity asked.

"January fifth. It will take around sixteen days to travel the six hundred or so kilometres to the lake, which will put us there around the twenty-first or so. This will give us enough time before the January thirtieth crossing start."

"The thought of sitting in a cave for up to six days is a joke," Trinity said.

"Joke, yes, but nothing I can do." With that, Jacob left Trinity and headed down inside the ship to eat and rest.

The plan was simple, or Jacob hoped it would be. They would leave on January fifth, ride for sixteen days to the lake, and wait until around the twenty-ninth. Then they would sail out to the caves, enter, and wait. The crew would wait six days. If the two families did not return, the crew was ordered to return to the *Semper Fi* and set sail to Cozumel, New Spain. There they would wait until Trinity, Jacob, Keara, Tom, and the children returned.

To the captain and crew, this was madness. But, it was not their place to ask why; it was to do as they were told.

That night, Jacob sat with his family and friends. The eight were all gathered together, sitting in the mess hall of the ship. Jacob sat before them now as a schoolteacher, a commander in chief.

"What we are about to do will not be easy on you, especially you young ones. The days will be hot, nights cold, and we only have so much food and water."

Bianca and Christopher sat there looking at their father. "We are ready, Father," Bianca said. "We will follow you to the ends of the earth, as Mamá would say."

"Thank you, Bianca. In the coming month, you will be tested. All of you will be tested." Jacob pointed at all of them.

"I was hoping we were past all this. I thought for sure we were done moving, looking for the next hill to cross," Keara replied.

"So did I. Three years was enough," Trinity said.

"Three long years," Keara added.

December 24, 1754

Christmas Eve aboard the *Semper Fi*. The sun was still high in the sky as Captain Correa gave a short Mass in the name of God the Father. They all gathered for this moment.

"Dios los bendiga a todos," Captain Correa said, which they all repeated thereafter.

"Amen," said Trinity as she made the sign of the cross.

That night, the eight sat around, and each exchanged one gift in private. It was now after midnight, and the children had fallen asleep. Trinity and Keara blew out the lanterns in their rooms and then went up on deck to join Jacob and Tom.

The sun was now starting to move down toward the horizon. Trinity climbed up onto the ship's rail and held on to the rigging. She stood there looking out at the bay around her. The only sound was the wind and the water touching the side of the ship. No one spoke. The four just stood there silently. Trinity thought back on her life.

"I can't remember any of the Christmases with my family anymore," she said.

"I can't remember my family. Their faces are just a shadow in my mind," Keara added.

Tom turned and looked at Keara.

"The waiting is the part I hate," Trinity added.

"Soon, Trinity. Life is a river. You can't push it. Everything has a time. You taught me that," Jacob said. He turned and pulled Trinity down from the rail and kissed her. "Merry Christmas."

January 1, 1755

The boredom of days at sea was now replaced by the boredom of sitting on a ship waiting for the day to leave. January 1, a New Year, one more year living in the past, one more year closer to the end. No one felt like celebrating the New Year. The only celebration was a glass of wine, a toast to 1755. In years past, the start of the New Year was filled with joy, excitement, and hope. But not this year. When they counted the days ahead, they saw things differently. Hope was replaced by sadness, disappointment. All that mattered now was to get home, say their good-byes from afar, and return to this time to wait for the last sunset.

The children played on the beach, running up and down the sand, laughing and exploring. Trinity slowly walked the beach barefoot. The waves washed across her feet; the water was cold. She thought back to the Orange River. Bianca was one and had just started to walk. Her first steps were on the sands of Africa. Now thirteen, she was a young lady. Soon she and her brother would be on their own. But for now, Trinity would make the most out of life.

God gives us only so much time, and we need to make the most of it.

January 5, 1755

Finally. At just after 1:00 p.m., the three wagons, boat, and eleven crew members in support departed Puerto San Julián. They rode down the main dirt street of the town, which led to the open desert. On each side were a number of mud buildings. In the lead was Jacob riding his horse. Next to him was Trinity, followed by Keara and Tom. They each wore white riding pants and high black boots. Trinity had on a large hat to protect her from the long, sunny days. In the wagons behind were Bianca, Christopher, Erich, and Josh. The wagons bounced over the rough ground, their cargo being thrown from one side to the other. Each wagon was loaded with the needed supplies to make the trek north to Bahía Jara, Chile Chico. The last wagon had a large wooden boat that would hold eight; it was pulled by four horses. The going from the start was slower than Jacob had hoped. He kept looking back at the last wagon, concerned by its slow progress.

By the end of the first day, they were thirty or so kilometres along, short of Jacob's forty-kilometre goal. They made camp and tried to get a few hours' sleep before starting out again.

Trinity put the children to sleep in the back of one of the wagons and then found a few minutes to sit down next to Jacob. "Always tomorrow. We can try to make up time," she said.

"I hope so," replied Jacob.

January 8, 1755

The group were now forced to head more north than Jacob had anticipated. The ground was just too hilly and rough. The horses could have made it, but not the wagons. Each day now, the children were walking next to the wagon. They found the ride just too rough for them. At other times, they would double up on the horses. Christopher would ride with Trinity and Bianca with Jacob. Keara and Tom, did the same, taking turns with their children.

January 14, 1755

The ground was now greening. Sandy rock gave way to clumps of green grass patches and desert shrubs. They were now halfway to what would be known as the Marble Caves. Every hour Jacob would pull his twenty-first-century compass and check their direction. Trinity rode alongside the wagon that held the wood trunk holding the slate computer and field gate generators. The trunk bounced from side to side. She worried that the equipment wouldn't survive the journey.

January 26, 1755

Finally the shores of Lake Carrera, Argentina. The water was breathtaking, clear blue. Around the lake to the north were snow-capped mountains. These mountains marked the border to Chile.

Their white clothes had now become dirt stained. Boots were marked and scratched from the rocks. They stopped and jumped from their horses, onto the black-sanded shore of the lake. The water was cold to the touch as the waves slowly washed ashore.

Trinity looked out to the lake. "It reminds me of the day we first came to the Pacific Ocean after walking three months to escape the winter."

"You still remember that day?" Jacob asked.

"That's the funny thing. I remember every day after we stepped into the past. In some cases, they are like yesterday. It's the days before we time travelled that are fading."

"Yes, I wonder if any of that is real anymore. Or was it just a dream, the first eighteen years of our lives?"

January 27, 1755

By nightfall, the two families made it to the border of Chile and Argentina, their final stop. From here they would have to use the boat to make the last ten-kilometre crossing to the Marble Caves on the north shore of the lake.

The time was just after midnight. The crew members stood alongside their employers looking out at the vast body of water. One could only guess the thoughts passing through their minds. Madness was most likely the only one that made sense to them.

"Way to go. Two days to spare. Good night," Keara said. She turned from the group and headed back to the wagons to sleep.

The children stood there looking out to the water. Erich looked over to Trinity, a look of confusion on his face, perhaps a look of questioning trust. Erich, like so many, was now wondering what his parents were up to.

Trinity looked at Erich. "A few more days and then you will see things you can't even imagine."

Erich smiled, but inside he questioned the things around him. Trinity and Keara made a point to teach their children to question all things, never take things at face value.

Jacob took Trinity's hand. "Love you, Trinity," he said. He always made a point to tell her he loved her each night before going to sleep, for no one knew what the following day would bring.

January 29, 1755

At noon, Jacob and Tom, with the help of the crew, pushed the boat into the water. Trinity, Keara, and the children boarded. There was six days' worth of food, and most importantly, the wood trunk with the computer and gates was placed safely in the centre.

Jacob, in Spanish, reiterated the plan to the crew. They were to wait seven days. If they did not return by the seventh day, they were to pick up camp and head back to the ship. Once there, they would tell the captain it was good to set sail for Cozumel, New Spain. There they would wait until late September for their return. If they did not return by October, they would set sail home to the Canary Islands without them.

The crew looked at Jacob. They understood, not knowing why they would do this, but they understood what they were to do.

"Gracias por toda su ayuda," Jacob said to all of them. With that, he and Tom climbed into the small boat and pulled out four oars. They each took one and gave the other two to Erich and Christopher.

Slowly they pushed off from the shore and started to row north-west across the lake. The children looked at their parents with a look of disbelief. Trinity's eyes were on the horizon. The prize was now less than twelve hours away.

Jacob worked at putting up the small sail, which would speed their crossing of the lake. With little to no wind, they would have to row hard to make the ten kilometres by night and the start of the gate cycle.

The crew waved their good-byes to these people, who, in their minds, they would never see again.

The lake was calm. The water was perfect for crossing. It was like the universe was opening the way for the journey to begin again.

Thank you, God, Trinity thought. *Thank you for once again looking after us and giving us the chance to do what is right. Thank you for the journey to this point.*

Chapter Six

The Marble Caves

By the night of January 29, the small boat and its passengers had crossed the lake. The wind had come up, and they were now sailing west along the north shore, looking for the Marble Caves.

Then at 1:30 a.m. on January 30, they came to a number of marble rock formations that dotted the coast. The long days of daylight gave them a chance to search for the right cave. Tensions were high. It was now after the marked start date, and between now and February 3, the gate could open. It was now almost two hours into the window.

Trinity looked to Jacob with a look of concern. "Which one?" she demanded.

Jacob opened the trunk and pulled out the slate computer. He opened it and logged into the machine. "Hold on one minute."

Time was now ticking away for them. Finally Jacob pulled out his monocular and looked around, searching. The cliffs around them were high. The rocks went straight up. There was no place to land a boat should they have to.

Just then, the yellow-orange moon rose from the horizon and climbed into the sky.

"There, over there, that set of rocks," Jacob said as he pointed to a towering rock cluster that sat out in the water by itself. By the base, they could see a number of holes, or caves, left by thousands of years of water erosion.

"You're kidding," Trinity said.

"No, start rowing!"

The men took hold of the paddles and started to row as quickly as they could toward the rock island. Within ten minutes, they touched the stone for the first time. They looked up at the tower above them. It reached to the sky. What concerned them, though, was not the sky but the caves below within the marble fortress. The cave walls made of marble were all round and curved. The stone was white and grey in color and swirled in all directions. The reflection from the water cast a blue hue over everything. The boat sailed into the caves and came to rest in a shallow area. Jacob and Tom jumped out and pulled the boat onto the smooth stone bottom.

"OK, this should be good," Jacob said.

The caves stretched only ten metres in any direction. From all sides they could see the open water through the spaces between the rocks.

"You're kidding. No way. Don't we have to be deep inside the earth for this to work?" Keara asked.

"I guess not. Now help me set up the field gates," Jacob said.

Tom opened the trunk, pulled out the three gates, and handed them to Jacob. He, in turn, started to set them up around the boat, in a triangle pattern, about three metres away from them. Jacob switched each of them on as he placed them, and they came to life with a warm blue glow from the top of each unit.

The children were left shocked.

"Mamá," Bianca said to Trinity.

"Not now, dear, not now!"

Once in place, Jacob took the slate computer and logged in again. He set the end date for March 10, 2016. There was a soft humming sound from each unit.

"There. Now we wait and hope we didn't miss it."

All eyes were on Jacob.

"While we wait, no one can leave the circle for the next five days." Jacob pointed to each of the children. "Got it? We are stuck here until something happens. Clear?"

Josh lifted his hand.

"Yes?"

"What happens if we have to go to pee?"

"You will have to do it within the circle."

"Great, just like the time we sailed down the coast of California and you got sick. You remember that, Trinity? You had diarrhea, and you had to go in the boat. You remember that?" Keara asked.

Trinity looked at her. "Yes, not one of my prouder moments."

"Let's get some sleep. It's late, and I hope to God that this happens in the next few days," Jacob said.

The group struggled to find some space in the small boat as they settled in for the night. The only sound was that of the field gates keeping them company in the dark.

January 30, 1755

All day they sat, waiting. Nothing. The children were losing their minds. They kept asking what was going to happen. To them, their parents were crazy, gone off the deep end. If not for the fact they were sitting on a stone island, they would have run off for sure. But, being water trapped kept them in place, waiting, asking over and over again. It got to the point that even Trinity and the others questioned if this was real or just some bad joke on the part of Markus.

Jacob looked at Trinity. "Read a book."

"I did. I finished them all a month ago."

"Listen to some music."

"I would, but it wouldn't be fair to the rest of you."

"Then close your eyes and try to sleep."

Trinity sat there staring at the gates and the computer. She looked at the children, who looked like they were being punished for misbehaving.

"Hang in there. Soon," Trinity whispered.

February 2, 1755

Jacob was eating and handing out food to the group.

"No thank you," Keara said. "I will only have to go to the toilet again, and I can't do that again in front of all of you."

"Oh," Jacob said.

Noon turned into evening. Then, as they sat there, there was a sound they had not heard in fifteen years.

Jacob, who was dozing off, awoke and looked around. He pulled himself up in the boat. There was a taste in his mouth. He looked around, frantic.

"Are we all here?" he yelled out.

"What?" Tom said.

"Bianca, Christopher, Erich, Josh!"

"Yes, we are all here…Oh my God. Do you hear it—and taste it?" Trinity said.

The sound got louder and louder. Bianca started to gag on the taste in her mouth. "Mamá!" she said.

"Hold on, dear!" Trinity looked to Erich and smiled at him. Erich smiled back.

Then there was a light, a greenish aurora light, that started to form around them. The sound became deafening. Bianca started to scream.

"*No!*" she called out.

Then, like fifteen years ago, the light enveloped them, taking their being their whole substance. Then it was gone.

Suddenly the boat, and the persons in the boat, found themselves surrounded by a metre-high wall of water that rushed in with a roar from all sides. The time shift had happened, and in the present day, the lake water was one metre higher than it was in 1755. The boat rose from the stone shelf it was sitting on and floated toward the ceiling of the cave. Jacob jumped from the boat and dove into the water, trying to rescue the field gate generators before they were lost. The water was cold and a shock to his system.

"Oh my God, Jacob!" screamed Trinity.

Jacob got the first gate and handed it to Tom. "Here, take it!" he yelled to him.

After a minute of trashing around in the water, Jacob recovered all three units and pulled himself into the boat again. The children looked at him in disbelief. Bianca slowly moved toward her father and hugged him.

Trinity looked to Jacob. "Way to go, dear, way to go." She smiled at him and started to laugh. "Yes, thank you, God!" she shouted.

Jacob packed the slate computer and the three gate generators once again in the trunk for safekeeping. Then they took the oars and slowly pushed their way clear of the marble island tower. The sun was bright and strong. They covered their eyes as they cleared the stone island; and tried to get their bearings in this new land.

"Are we in the right year?" Trinity asked.

"No clue," Jacob said with some hesitation. "See if your phone has a cell signal?"

Trinity looked, but there was no service.

They started to once again row north toward the northern bay. By the time the sun was setting behind the Andes Mountains, they made landfall at a small inlet with a long brown sand beach. They pulled the boat ashore and looked around.

"Do you know the day?" Trinity asked.

"Nope, no clue, could be plus or minus three days from what we hope to hit."

"Time?" Keara said as she stumbled out of the boat.

"No. Late, I would say."

Keara pushed her way past Jacob and the others. "Out of the way, need to find a bush."

Jacob started to walk up the beach, looking for any sign of life, when Tom called out, "Haven't seen one of these in fifteen years." He was holding a Coke can in his hand.

Trinity ran over. "Let me see!"

It was funny; a piece of garbage was of more value now than the diamonds of South Africa. The children walked up and looked at the strange object. Erich took it and was amazed by how light it was.

"What is it?" he asked.

"A can, a soda can," Tom said.

"What do you use it for?" Bianca asked.

"Well, you, uh…store soda in it."

"What is *soda*?" Christopher asked.

"Ah…the next few days are going to be overwhelming for you all."

Jacob called over to the group, "Over here!" He waved his hands down the beach for the group to head over toward him.

Trinity was the first to arrive. "What?"

There stretched out before them was a cement boat launch leading from the water and up to a gravel road that headed north. Trinity walked up the pad, but stopped short of stepping onto the roadway. She looked at it and turned back to the group.

"What are you waiting for?" yelled Keara.

Trinity turned and made the first step on the gravel road. She kneeled down and put her hand on the man-made surface. She looked up the road and followed it with her eyes as it disappeared into the distance.

That night, the eight sat around a fire to stay warm. The last four days in the cave with no good food or warmth had been hard on each of them. But now they could stretch out beside the fire and rest, keep warm, and think about what tomorrow would bring.

Unknown day.

At first light, they were on the road walking northwest. Jacob and Tom carried the wood trunk between them. Trinity and the others had small backpacks made of off-white canvas. They were filled with enough items to last a few more days. If anyone would have come along, they would have seen eight very dirty, odd-looking people who did not belong in this time. They walked all day, not once coming across a single car.

"What the hell? Not a single car," Tom said.

"What's a car?" Erich asked.

"You'll know one when you see it," Tom replied to his son.

By late afternoon, they stopped at the side of the road and spotted a town off in the distance. The road was going away from the town, so the group decided to leave the road and head cross-country to the town.

As they walked, they finally came to the shore of the lake again and started to follow the shoreline toward the town. They came to a river, which stopped their progress. Just on the other side was the twenty-first century, so close, but still not within reach. Working their way north again along the river, they found a shallow spot to cross. The eight stepped into the cold mountain water and crossed, being careful not to fall with the wood trunk. Finally on the far side, they stopped and dumped the water from their boots.

They carried on, once again coming to the main road. Then suddenly, a car drove past them at high speed. Erich just stopped and froze.

"That, my boy, is a car," Tom said to his son.

"Where are the horses?" Erich asked.

"Under the hood."

"The hood?"

They came to a sign that read: Puerto Ingeniero Ibáñez. More cars raced by them. Not a single one slowed or gave them a second glance. They continued to walk down the main street of the town. People were now everywhere. The children were looking at the world in wonder. Some people would slow and look at them as if they were characters from a town play or festival.

"Mamá, why are they looking at us so strangely?" Bianca asked.

Christopher stepped in. "Because, stupid, they have never seen anyone from La Palma."

"In the next few days, you will start to understand what has happened to us. For now, just enjoy the new sights," Trinity said.

The small town was quite beautiful compared to the sights they had seen for the last month crossing the desert.

At the end of the street, they stopped, and Trinity started to ask people where there was a hotel or inn where they could spend the night. An old man walking his dog looked at them and then pointed down the road, saying there was an inn, but was not sure they would have room. Summer was very busy.

Trinity thanked him, and they started to walk, to the inn.

There at the end of the street was the two-story inn the old man had mentioned. They entered the small hotel and rang the bell in the front lobby. A native South American–looking woman entered and was shocked to see the guests she had standing in her company.

"¿Nos puede ayudar? Necesitamos una habitación." Trinity said, asking for a room.

The woman looked at them, and said, "Sí," but asked how they would pay. "Efectivo o crédito?"

Jacob reached into his bag, pulled out a gold coin, and placed it on the counter before the shocked woman. She looked at it and then at them. She finally picked it up and looked very closely at it.

She asked in Spanish, "Is it real?"

"Sí," Jacob responded, nodding his head.

The woman smiled and then slid a piece of paper across the desk for them to fill in. Trinity looked at it and then dropped her pack to the floor. The woman handed her a pen. Trinity looked at it and started to write, but at first she could not get the hang of it. Fifteen years of using a quill was very different to using a pen.

Trinity turned to Jacob. "Address?"

"La Palma," he said.

After Trinity filled in the form, the woman took it and asked them to follow her. She took them down a short hall to two rooms across from each other. The door to the room swung open, and they entered. The room was plain, with furniture from the seventies. In any century, the only word that could be used to describe it was "ugly," but there were two beds, and for tonight, they would do.

Jacob asked if there was a bank in town where he could exchange gold coins. The woman paused and then told him there was only one bank on Main Street.

The children looked at the room, then looked in the bathroom and started to ask questions about it. Trinity told them to be quiet for minute.

Jacob turned back to the woman and asked one last thing of her, what the date was. "¿Cual es la fecha?"

She responded March fourteenth. He then asked the year. The woman paused and looked at him. She laughed and then said, "2016."

"Excelente," Jacob replied.

That night, the two families slept peacefully in their own rooms. Trinity slept with Jacob by her side and her two children in the bed next to them.

After being gone for fifteen years, they were now on the road home.

March 15, 2016

At first light, Jacob and Trinity left the hotel, walked to the bank, and waited for it to open. At nine thirty the doors to Banco de Chile opened, and they entered. By eleven, they left the bank with $1 million Chilean pesos, about US$2,400, after selling one gold coin and a lot of explaining, which consisted of 90 percent lies. Did they get the best deal? No. But they had pesos to move on to Santiago and the gold and diamond exchanges of the big city.

They returned to the hotel, got their belongings, said thank you, and went for lunch. By two thirty, they boarded a bus that would take them north to Coyhaique. Three hours later, they stepped off the bus into a small town of forty-five thousand people in the mountains of Chile. Compared to the last month, the hills were green with life.

They started to walk the streets and finally found a hotel at the west side of the town. Then the eight went out and shopped for clothes to match the world around them. Trinity and Keara were amazed by the beautiful clothing and the different styles. Tom and Jacob tried on men's clothing. The children found the whole thing out of this world.

The concept of time travel was not mentioned to the children, so to them, this world was a far-off kingdom in a land far away, a magical trek so hard that people would not risk their lives to make this journey. The children were excited to see all the unusual clothes and shoes. The fabrics were so strange to them. Erich stopped and picked up a watch and looked at it. It was black and orange with a number of hands and dials.

"What is this?" Erich asked.

Jacob came over. "A watch like the one I have." He pulled out his pocket watch. "They do the same thing, but this one fits on your wrist."

"Can I have one?"

"Yes, Erich."

"Gracias." Erich said, thanking him.

That night they left the shop, looking like twenty-first-century travellers, perhaps not with the best taste in style, but they now fit in to their new surroundings. Next they went and purchased new backpacks and a large padded bag to place the slate computer and gates in for safe-keeping.

And so ended their second day in this new, yet old world for Trinity and her friends. They felt great. After a fabulous dinner, they returned to their hotel to rest and plan for the coming days.

March 16, 2016

The day started out with a number of problems. After breakfast, they tried to figure out how to make it to Santiago. When Jacob first came up with his plan, he thought there would be bus service that would take them north to the capital of Chile. But, it turned out there was no bus that ran in Chile. The buses needed to go into Argentina first and then back into Chile farther north.

With no passports, they could not cross the border between the two countries. The only option was for them to fly out from Coyhaique Airport. But, again, they would need ID for this. The good news was passports should not be needed. Jacob pulled from his bag the IDs he had kept for the last fifteen years for Trinity, Tom, Keara and himself. They were yellow and old looking, and the people in the photos did not look much like the people today. Fifteen years can change a person a lot.

"What about ID for the children?" Trinity asked.

"We will have to tell them we were robbed and lost everything. With some begging and cash, we should be able to get on the plane and fly north."

"The kids will go crazy when they get on the plane and fly for the first time," Keara said.

"Yes, I can hardly wait to see that," Trinity responded.

There was one more trip to a bank to change one more gold coin. This time they received almost $2 million pesos, double from the last bank. Then they were off to the shops for a good suitcase that would hold the gates and computer safely.

After this, Trinity and Jacob took a cab to the airport to try to book tickets for the eight. The cab pulled up to the small airport building with a dark grey roof and a small control tower next to it. They asked the driver to wait for them.

The only airline they could use was LAN. They entered the building and made their way to the desk. The place was dead. No one was around at the time, only a single man at the ticket desk.

"Disculpe. ¿Nos podría ayudar?" Trinity asked if the man could help them.

They went on to book the eight seats on the plane for Santiago. Cash got them the seats, but when it came to the IDs, things slowed down. After an hour of talking back and forth, with the supervisor being called, they were able to work a deal. But, they would have to be on the noon flight tomorrow since this was the time the supervisor would be on shift again to get them on the plane. They thanked the supervisor and left. Still waiting outside was the cab driver, reading his newspaper.

"Well, that went well," Trinity said to Jacob.

In fact, their actions had opened the door to the Gatekeepers of the future. Little did they know their actions would send a message to the future. It would take three hundred years to get there, but time is irrelevant if you can cross it.

That day, at 4:33, eight names went into a computer at the LAN Airlines desk. The first was Trinity Warner Kennedy, followed by Jacob Kennedy, and then the others. This single action would put everything ahead of them at stake.

Chapter Seven

The Origins

June 2337

In the Andaman Sea sat islands of towering rocks that reached skyward two hundred feet straight up, like fingers to heaven. At the base of one of these towers of stone was an entrance to an underground lab. A short airstrip leading from the beach made its way to its base. The main doors led into a great white-and-black hall standing three stories high and five hundred feet long. On each side of the great hall were towering graphene computers, which were liquid, cooled from a river of water that ran down the centre of the hall; the massive computers held all of the world's knowledge. They acted like pillars that held up the cathedral-like ceiling. From the tops of the great computer columns, vines hung down toward the floor. Crossing the river were a number of bridges from one side to the other. At the far end were ascending balconies that climbed up toward the ceiling, and off of each balcony was a wall of glimmering glass.

Behind these windows were the Gatekeepers, a twenty-fourth-century monk-like order who dressed in white robes. They sat at desks made of glass, looking at holographic displays. All the knowledge that was, and would be coming in the future, would find itself here in time.

On the highest level of the great hall sat an office, reserved for the master Gatekeeper, known only as KA. In a room the size of a small auditorium was a single desk. Behind it sat KA. He surveyed his world around him and below him from his vantage point. KA was entrusted with the protection of the universe, past and future. Everything had a place, an order in the universe, and the Gatekeepers would see to this order.

KA sat at his desk, listening to soft epic music. He rested there with little emotion. On each side of him, there were holographic screens conveying information.

A Gatekeeper dressed in a red robe entered his domain; he carried a small black graphene pad. He approached KA, bowing his head, and spoke. "Master KA."

KA looked up from his desk and gazed at the man. "Yes?"

"There has been a change in the recorded time-line," the red-robed man said.

"Markus!"

KA lifted his hand, gesturing for the man to give him the pad. The red-robed man handed it to KA.

KA studied it. "What is the change we are seeing?"

"The Origins have left the seventeen hundreds and returned to their own time."

"What? No!"

"Trinity and those close to her are now in 2016. They have left the first indications of their being on the data stream."

As the men talked, a second man wearing a grey robe walked into the room. "If what I am hearing is true, all that is and will be is in danger of being destroyed," he said.

"History records the death of Trinity and Jacob in 1757 and 1758. To maintain the order of all, they cannot exist outside this time."

"Markus must have made contact with them and provided them with the means," the red-robed man said.

KA stood and turned from his desk and looked out the window to the hall below. "Where are they now?"

"Southern Chile, 2016. We know their names appeared on an LAN Airlines booking database."

"Are there any more indications?"

"No. This is the first."

The grey-robed man stepped forward and approached KA. "Master, to protect all that is and will be, they must die!"

KA turned and looked at him. "Yes, they must." He looked at the red robe. "Can we summon a team to deal with them?"

The red-robed man walked forward and picked up the pad from KA's desk. He looked at it. "No, the only windows to cross are not within the area they are in now in Chile. We would have to use our island lab to push a crossing to the 2016 time era. Based on the push from this location, the team will not make it there on time before they move on. We will need them to move on and come to another control point. Once we have a more precise location, the team can intercept them."

"How long before more information will be coming forward?" KA asked.

The red robe looked down to his pad. "Wait, it is already starting to come in. The communication device Trinity used has linked to a system that was known as iCloud via the Wi-Fi Internet of the time and streamed an archive of photos to the main server."

"The phone! Where are they?"

"Unclear, in 2016, we would only know the town they are in in southern Chile, but not the exact location yet."

"Nothing can happen to the phone unit. It must be returned to the 1750s so the children of Trinity and Keara can pass on the messages it holds. It is key to the future," KA said.

"We will see to it. No harm will come of the communication unit. We will safeguard it, and see to the end of the four, to guard the timeline."

"Good, ready your assassination team. They are to leave in the next window to 2016. Tell them we will have all the knowledge needed to intercept the Origins and kill them!" KA said.

The grey robe spoke. "The next window is not slated until three cycles from now. They must be stopped at once!"

KA snapped at the man, "What do you want us to do? We cannot cross until the sun is right and the gate can be opened. You are to blame for this; you granted Markus the chance to save his wife. Now, because of your weakness, you have placed all in danger, an end to this timeline—and us."

The red-robed man bowed his head to KA.

"Ready the team. Tell them failure is not an option," KA said.

The two robes stepped back, bowed, and turned to leave. KA stood there with a look of pure anger on his face. He once again turned and looked at the great hall below. He would not let his empire be threatened by people who lived five hundred years ago.

"Damn you, Markus. Damn you. How dare you bring in the Origins into all this."

Seated in a white room with lush green plants and trees interspersed sat six men and four women. Each wearing a white robe; some had their hoods upon their heads as they sat studying historic data. The red-robed man entered and walked over to them.

A man by the name of Gustavo looked up. Pulling his hood from his head, he looked at him. He paused and then said, "You have come to tell me that I now have to kill my brother."

"No, your brother is still nowhere to be found in the timeline. He still hides in a time before which we can track him. We need you and your brother- and sisterhood to end the life of the Origins."

Gustavo turned his head to the side, thinking, and looked up at the ceiling. "How can we kill the Origins? All that is, is because of them."

"Yes, but they have wandered from their time and are now in danger of changing all events. This is the doing of Markus."

Gustavo sat there looking at the red robe. "When do we leave?"

"In three weeks. By then we will have all their control points noted. We will be able to find a crossing point close to a date that will work for you."

Gustavo stood and looked at the others in the room. They all slowly stood, pushing their chairs back.

"Three weeks will be more than enough time."

"Are you clear that the Origins are to die?" the red robe asked.

"Very clear. We will execute with extreme prejudice, for the sake of the timeline now and in the future," Gustavo said.

"Only the four must die. There cannot be any other deaths. Are you clear? We have no way of knowing how it will affect things. Are you clear on this?"

The men and women started to file out of the room, leaving the red robe standing alone.

Just as Gustavo was the last to leave the room, the red-robed man called out, "Do not fail me, Gustavo."

Gustavo stopped, paused, and then kept walking. "I am not my brother," he said.

Chapter Eight

Santiago

March 17, 2016

The twin-engine LAN aircraft came in low over the vineyards north of Santiago International Airport. Erich looked from the window of the plane and continued to be speechless as he saw the wonders of his life unfolding these last few days.

Erich asked, "Father, why do these people not use these flying machines, as you call them, to travel to our home of La Palma? Why did we have to embark on such a hard journey by sea, then by land, to come here, when this is a much better way to travel?"

Tom looked at his oldest son. "You are a smart boy, you know that? In the coming days, we will try and help you understand what has happened to you, to all of us."

Bianca and Christopher sat in their seats and looked out the windows. Like Erich and Josh, they were overwhelmed by what was happening. Trinity and Jacob, who had the aisle seats, looked over to their children and smiled at the looks on their faces. Very quickly they were accepting the new world around them, much better than they had hoped.

The flight crew came over the intercom and told the passengers to fasten their seat belts for landing. Bianca looked around, somewhat confused. Trinity leaned over and checked her seat belt.

"Sit back, dear, and enjoy. We will be on the ground again very soon," Trinity said.

Just after 3:00 p.m., the plane touched down at the Santiago International Airport and slowed to taxi to the east side of the terminal. There the plane came to a stop some distance from the main building. The engines shut down, and the side door swung down onto the tarmac. The eight unstrapped themselves and waited to deplane. After they left the aircraft, they stopped and picked up their luggage as it was placed beside the plane. Jacob took the case with the gates and computer.

Trinity and Keara stood there looking in disbelief at the sights before them. Trinity said, "I was here eighteen years ago."

Jacob corrected her. "Actually Dear, you were here five years ago. It's 2016, and you were last here in 2011."

They made their way onto a bus that took them to the main terminal. There they found themselves standing in the arrival hall, lost.

"Now what?" Trinity asked.

"Don't know, never thought we would make it this far," Jacob said.

"We did."

"I guess get a car."

"Taxis should be on the lower level," Trinity said.

"I mean a rental car."

Trinity looked at Jacob with a look of disbelief.

Tom stepped in. "Why? Why not get a cab?"

"Because I want a car. I want to be able to go where I want when I want. Do we have a problem with that?" Jacob said, raising his voice.

"A car? You still know how to drive? The last thing I saw you ride was a horse for the last thirteen years," Tom replied.

"I don't think they rent horses, so a car will have to do!"

Trinity looked at him with a look of "You're an idiot. But, whatever."

They made their way to the rental car desks, and after an hour with the staff, dealing with questions like why their faces did not match their Alberta driver's licences anymore, plus leaving a $4,000 deposit for the rental, they were finally able to get a van.

"We could have gotten a taxi and left an hour ago," Trinity said.

Jacob walked straight ahead, ignoring them all.

They left the building and made their way to the rental car area on the east side of the airport. Standing there was a white 2013 Nissan van with dented side-door panels. Jacob stopped and looked at it.

"Well, someone has got a good start on it; anything you add should not show too bad," Tom said to Jacob.

"Pound sand, Wilde!"

The rental car person went over the van and asked for someone to sign. They all looked at Jacob.

The eight piled into the vehicle. Jacob sat behind the wheel, then looked at the dash and then down at the stick shift. "Shit, a standard!"

"We're going to die," Keara said.

"No, not here, not now. Our place to die is back home, when the time comes," Trinity said.

"I guess it is nice knowing your last day. Makes you feel invincible knowing nothing can happen to you yet." Keara said.

The four children, crowded in the back, and immediately started to complain it was too hot and they needed more room in the wagon.

"You got to love married life and children," Trinity said. She turned and yelled at the children in Spanish, "Cállense y pórtense bien!"

"What the hell is it, three days into the twenty-first century, and they sound like every other whiny kid?" Keara said.

"We were never like that."

"I bet your parents would disagree with you," Keara finished.

Jacob started the van, and slowly, with a few jerks, they were off into the Santiago traffic on a weekday. God help them.

It was just after 6:00 p.m. now as they left the airport for central Santiago. The sun was just starting to set over the city. Trinity acted as navigator, because she knew Santiago well. However, that was eighteen years ago for her. They headed east on Costanera to Kennedy.

Trinity looked up at the street sign and said, "Look, a street named after you."

Finally they came across a large shopping mall on the right side of the road.

"Stop!" Trinity demanded.

Jacob rolled his eyes and did as he was told. "You're kidding."

Jacob pulled into the parkade, and as he did, he saw the Marriott hotel next door.

Tom looked at him. "Think they have room?"

"One can hope."

"By the way, good driving, guy."

"Thank you. Took a bit, but it's coming back."

The eight made their way into the glass megamall of towering steel. There were large neon billboards projecting videos and sales ads. The children just wandered around, walking into everything. Their minds were so lost in what they saw, the people, and the stores. It was all too overwhelming. Bianca broke down and started to cry. Trinity came to her and held her tight.

"Mamá, I can't do this. It's too much."

"Shhh, yes, you can. Look at me. It's OK, dear. Stay close to me. Tonight, before you go to bed, I am going to tell you and Christopher a story about who your mother and father really are."

Bianca looked at her.

"But first I need to find something."

Trinity walked a few more minutes with the others in tow. Then she came to what she was looking for, an Apple store.

"There you are," Trinity said.

Jacob followed her.

She walked in and started to look at the iPhones. An hour later, she and the others left. Trinity had a new iPhone, and she had the salesperson move over all her files from her old iPhone to her new one. She also had two new SLXtreme cases to protect them for the next 270 years. Her old phone was safely cleaned and a new battery placed inside by the staff. It was then packed in a box for safekeeping.

"Trinity, you know that's cheating," Jacob said to her.

"Is it? I am making sure my message gets home when the time comes."

From the mall, they walked next door to the Marriott hotel and booked two suites. Trinity filled out the room cards, and Jacob placed down the needed pesos to cover the rooms for the next week. The hotel staff then took their bags and showed them to their rooms.

Later that night, just after nine, the eight sat down for dinner at the main restaurant atop the Marriott Hotel. From the top floor, they could look out over Santiago . The view was breathtaking. The children stood at the window, looking out at all the lights. They just stood there. Not a single child said anything. Their eyes were wide. They watched as the lights from the cars drove down below on the streets.

Jacob made sure that all the wineglasses were filled. He then lifted his glass and made a toast. He looked out the window at the city lights in the hills around the city. It reminded him of Mazatlán 1740.

"To us, to being on the road home," Jacob said.

"To us." Then Trinity added, "To my loving friends, we have been through so much. To lost friends who did not make it home, you will always be missed!" There was a moment of silence as they sat there.

"Hear, hear," Jacob said.

They all took a drink of wine and smiled at each other.

"To friends," Keara said.

Later that night, they returned to their two-bedroom suites. The children were tired and went straight to bed. Trinity kissed each of them and made sure they were safe in their room. The four adults then retreated to the lounge at the top of the hotel.

For the next few hours, they sat there talking about how things were, the things they now missed, the things they didn't miss.

Jacob asked Trinity, "Why aren't you taking any photos of this with your new phone?"

"Because this never happened."

In the coming days, they would look to sell a few more of the gold coins and perhaps one or two diamonds to get money for the next part of their journey. But first, they would somehow need to acquire passports to travel in the twenty-first century. This would turn out to be a great challenge, and they would rely on the goodness of people and their hearts to make it happen.

Just after midnight, Trinity and Jacob lay down in bed. Jacob held Trinity tightly. The only light was from the moon shining into the bedroom. Jacob kissed Trinity with a passion that had been missing for the last few years. That night, they made love, but very quietly.

March 18, 2016

They all met for breakfast in Trinity and Jacob's room. The hotel staff rolled in a tray filled with all sorts of fine food—artisan breads, organic cheese, gourmet coffee, and more.

After breakfast, Bianca came to her mother and sat down beside her. "You told me you were going to tell me a story of who you are and who I am?"

Trinity looked at her. "I did." Then she looked to Keara.

Keara turned and called her children. "Erich, Josh, come here please. Trinity is going to tell us a story, a story you are old enough to know now and one you may find hard to believe."

The four children took their places on the couch across from Trinity. Jacob and Tom sat down on the windowsill.

Trinity started into the journey of her and her friends' lives. She told them where she was born, how she had lived in Canada, and what happened to them in the Chungo Caves that March 24, 2014.

She told them how Robert died, who the first people were to find them and save their lives. How they sailed to New Spain and met a kind, loving friar who took them into his church in love. How a man by the man of Don Carlos took pity on them and gave them a chance, who found the love to take them into his family. How because of the love of family she needed to send a message home to her loved ones. How on the way to Europe they were attacked by the British and how Kim, a loving friend, was killed by a bullet through the heart.

How they went to Cuba and how a man by the name of Francisco watched over them until it was time to leave. How their friend Andy disappeared in the night, never to be seen again. The loss of the *San Ingnacio* by fire and how it broke their hearts seeing the ship slip below the waves. How they left Cuba for Spain, Amsterdam, South Africa, and the Orange River.

How a loving French family in Cape Town once again took them in, where Bianca was born, where Erich was born. How they almost lost their lives on the beach of the Orange River, how a Bushman named Shapipa saved her life and that of Keara.

How they returned to Lisbon as poor travellers, but once there claimed their wealth from the diamonds they had, and finally how they found everlasting peace on La Palma Island.

And how proud she was of her and Keara's children for being who they were, who they had become.

Bianca and the others sat there for close to an hour listening to Trinity. At times the children would start to cry, but then their hearts would be lifted again.

Finally Bianca turned to her mother and said. "Mamá, you and Father are time travellers."

Trinity turned to all present. "Yes, as hard as it is to believe, we are just that. The first, but not the last. You sitting here in front of me are the children of time travellers; you were given a gift, an edge, over all those around you. Use it wisely. Use it for good."

Bianca stood up and ran toward her mother, hugging her as she started to cry. The other children followed, one by one, and lovingly embraced their parents.

So the secret was passed on to the children of the time travellers.

Late that afternoon, Trinity and Jacob made their way into the centre of Santiago, to a high-end gold coin exchange off of San Pablo Street.

As they got to the front door, a guard buzzed them into the showroom. An older man in his late fifties came to see how he could help. Trinity and Jacob said they had some gold coins to sell, and the man said he looked forward to seeing them.

He led them to his desk and asked them to sit. Jacob pulled out a small red bag and poured out six gold Spanish coins, pieces of eight. All had different dates, ranging from 1739 to 1751. As one would guess, they were like new, mint! The man's eyes went wide as he looked at each one. He weighted each and then pulled out a book to look them up.

Trinity and Jacob looked at each other, smiling. The man then asked to be excused as he went to make a phone call. At this point, Jacob started to get nervous. Then, after ten minutes, the man returned and apologised for taking so long.

Trinity said no problem.

The man said he would give them US$30,000 for the set. Trinity looked to Jacob.

"That should cover a few expenses for the next few weeks," she said.

Jacob said, "33,000 y tenemos un trato."

The man countered. "32,000."

Jacob said, "Sí, tienes un trato." He stood and shook the man's hand. The deal was done. $32,000 would go a long way.

The man left the shop and returned a short time later with a certified money order for the amount of $32,000.

Trinity and Jacob left the shop, money order in hand, and headed down the street to the bank the funds came from. They entered and sat down in front of the manager, asking for their cash. They were told the bank did not have that kind of money on hand and it would take a few days to get. But, the manager offered to set up a bank account and give them a debit card to access the funds. In the end, they needed more ID to open the account, so they left to return in the next few days to get their cash once it was on hand. That was unless they could find the needed ID the bank had requested.

As they stepped onto the street, Jacob gave the money order to Trinity and asked her to take it and place it in her purse. "There you go. Take care of it please. Don't lose it!"

"Now where to?" Trinity asked.

"I think back to the hotel. Tomorrow we need to go to the German embassy and see what we can manage there."

"Still not clear how you plan to pull that one off."

"You better hope we pull it off. If not, we are going to be stuck in Chile for a very long time."

March 19, 2016

First thing in the morning, they walked over to the German embassy, which was located on Las Hualtatas, a few blocks from the hotel. As they approached the white-and-red building, a guard came out and looked at them and asked what they needed. Trinity said they had been in an accident and all their *Reisepasses* were lost and they needed new ones.

The guard shook his head and opened the gate to let them in. They made their way into the building. After waiting a while in line, a woman finally came out and met them. Trinity retold the story, and the woman left, only to return with a man by the name of Klaus Gerber. He was a man in his forties, grey suit, a stuffy-looking man.

Trinity turned to Jacob and spoke to him softly in English. "We're screwed. You know that?"

"Time will tell," Jacob replied.

Klaus took them into his office on the main floor. He asked the *kinder* to wait outside. Tom and Keara said they would wait with the kids and Trinity and Jacob could go first.

"Good luck," Keara said.

Klaus closed the door. In Spanish, Trinity once again told the story how the passports were all lost when their luggage went missing.

Klaus understood and said he would help. But first, he needed Trinity's fingerprint to find her in the database. Trinity looked to Jacob as she moved to a fingerprint reader and put her fingers down on the glass.

"*Danke*," Klaus said.

"Do you speak English?" Trinity asked.

"Yes, why?"

"Can we speak English with you?"

"Yes, I have no problem with that," Klaus said. "This will only take a few minutes." He worked the mouse of the computer. He looked at the screen, and then at Trinity, then back to the screen. "Your passport was issued in 2013?"

"Yes, sounds about right."

Klaus turned the screen of the computer around so Trinity could see it. "This is you?"

There on the screen was a photo of Trinity at the age of sixteen years. Trinity was now thirty-three years old. Klaus looked at her.

"Is this you?"

"Yes, why?"

"When was this photo taken?"

"The last one was back in 2013, I think, when I got the last passport. But that one you see there is when I was sixteen, I think. Not sure why you have that one on file?"

Klaus nodded his head and turned the screen around again. He then asked Jacob to step forward so he could have his fingerprints. Jacob did it, but before he put his hand down, he already knew the outcome.

Klaus waited and then said, "I cannot find you in the system?"

Trinity then spoke up. "You see, here is the thing."

Klaus sat back in his chair.

"Jacob here is Canadian, but we've been married for the last thirteen years. And now have two children. I was hoping we could get passports for Jacob and my two children as Germans," Trinity said.

Klaus looked at her. "Do you have a marriage certificate?"

Trinity looked to Jacob. He pulled from his pocket a parchment from Mazatlán, New Spain and handed it over to Klaus.

Klaus looked at it. He then looked up at them. "You're kidding me. This is dated 1740. The names are right, but come on!"

"Must be a mistake on the part of the priest who did it," Trinity said.

"And your passport photo, it says you were born in 1996."

"There must be some mistake. How could I be born in 1996? Look at me. I am…" Trinity turned to Jacob. "How old am I?"

"Thirty-three," Jacob said.

"I'm thirty-three," Trinity repeated.

Klaus said, "We are Germans. We do not make mistakes." He sat back in his chair, looking at them. "Your fingerprint says you are Trinity Warner." He then pointed to Jacob. "You, I have no clue who you are. But you sit here asking for all-new German passports. I think not."

Trinity spoke up. "We need your help. We need passports so we can travel out of Chile. We need to get back to Canada to see my family who lives there."

Jacob pulled a small red bag from his pocket and placed it on the desk before Klaus.

"What is this?" Klaus dumped out two diamonds on the desk top. They were exquisite stones, with a value of over $30,000 each. "Are you trying to bribe me?"

"*No*, I am trying to save my family's life. And to do that, we need passports. Trinity is German, right? And being German, she can have a new passport. I am her husband, and therefore, I have the right to a passport. My children sitting out there have a right to a passport!"

"First, you have no rights. A passport is a privilege that we can take away at any time, Mr. Kennedy!" Klaus said.

Jacob sat back in the chair.

"Now leave my office and wait outside while I decide what I am going to do with you."

Trinity and Jacob stood. "Please, we need your help. I have not seen my parents in fifteen years. I need to see them again."

"Out," Klaus said.

They left the office and closed the door behind them. They sat in the outer office, waiting.

"Well, that went well," Keara said.

For the next hour they sat in the outer office, looking at the glass partition between them and Klaus's office. Behind the glass, Klaus could be seen on the phone, computer, and back on the phone again. He stood walked around and then sat down, looking back at the eight sitting in the outer room.

Finally, the door opened, and Klaus called Trinity, Jacob, Keara, and Tom in. The children were to wait.

They made their entry.

"Sit," Klaus said.

They all found a chair and sat down.

Pointing to Keara and Tom, Klaus said, "I assume you two will also be needing passports for your family, or otherwise, why would you be here?"

"Yes," Tom said.

"I do not know what is going on here. But I have looked you up on the Internet, Miss Warner. Your father, Carl, and mother, Maria, are the CEOs of Warner-Kennedy Corp., one of the largest privately owned companies in the world."

Trinity looked shocked. She turned to Jacob and the others.

"Your net worth is over one hundred billion."

"Way to go, Trinity," Jacob said to her under his breath.

"I do not know how you have been hiding in Chile for these last thirty-three years. But, since you are a German citizen, I will help you, Trinity." Klaus turned his attention to Keara and Tom. "Since you are not, but part of this mess anyway, I will also help you. But, I need valid marriage certificates from all of you, to make this somewhat legal"

Klaus pulled out a piece of paper and handed it to Trinity. "This is the name of a priest I know very well. I have spoken to him already. He will marry you again in a Chilean service tonight. He will then give you marriage certificates I can use, that prove you are married, and then I will try and get the needed passports for all of you."

They sat there quietly, shaken by the good fortune coming their way. Klaus tossed the red bag with the diamonds in it back to Jacob.

"You may need this more than I do," Klaus said.

"Thank you. Is there anything we can do for you?" Trinity asked.

"Perhaps someday, Miss Warner."

"How long before we get the passports?"

"Once I have your marriage documents in hand, and photos, we should have all the passports in five or six days from Germany."

Trinity stood and looked at Klaus. "You remind me of a kind and loving man who died a long time ago. He helped us. He saved us. *Danke schön.*"

"You are welcome, Frau Warner-Kennedy," Klaus said.

That night, Trinity, Jacob, Keara, and Tom met with Father Christos of the Iglesia San Francisco, a stone-and-mud church dating back to 1622 that had survived countless earthquakes over the last three hundred years. Christos knew they were coming and why, and he let them into the main church for the evening service. Afterward, worshipers from the 6:00 p.m. service remained seated. Some slowly started to file out. Some stayed and wanted to be part of the ceremony.

Just before 7:00 p.m., as the sun set on Santiago, with the candles burning all around them, Trinity, Jacob, Keara, and Tom were married again, this time in the year 2016.

> *I thought back to the last fifteen years of my life, the fifteen years which I spent with Jacob, and thought how lucky I was. I was blessed to have him by my side. Yes, at times we would fight. It is part of marriage; it is part of life. But, he loved me, and I loved him. We were at each other's side, looking out for one another. Life had given us an amazing journey. God had given us each other, and tonight, I was proud and happy to be married again to the man of my dreams. Thank you, God.*

They each said their vows again in Spanish, and after ten minutes, with their children looking on, Christos once again pronounced them man and wife. They each turned and looked into the other's eyes.

"Te amo," Trinity said.

"Love you too, dear."

They kissed and hugged each other. The children threw rice at them. Christos got mad and told them to stop, for now he would have to clean the church again at this late hour.

As they stood at the door of the church, saying their good-byes, Christos handed them their marriage documents. They thanked the priest and started to walk back to the hotel, a walk that was just over ten kilometres, but no one was in a rush tonight. They just wanted to walk in the fall evening air of this magical city in South America.

March 25, 2016

Easter Sunday for Santiago. The city was quiet as the people celebrated. Trinity and the others waited for news of their new passports, which would free them from the borders of Chile and provide them the means home.

That morning, as Trinity sat looking out the window from her hotel room, she turned and looked at the room phone. She stood and picked up her iPhone and started to look through the old phone numbers, which had not been used in years.

Finally she found the number she was looking for. It was her home number, a number she could no longer remember in her mind.

She picked up the receiver and slowly dialed the number. She pushed each button slowly, as if trying to justify the actions in her mind.

After a few seconds, the phone on the other end started to ring.

In Calgary, Alberta, Canada, in a kitchen in a spacious Spanish-design home, a phone rang. The time was just after 10:00 a.m. A housekeeper was putting dishes away; she stopped doing her task and turned to answer the phone. But just then, a teenage girl, fifteen years old, walked into the room. She had long hair and hazel eyes. She wore blue jeans and a white blouse and looked very much like Trinity did at seventeen.

"I'll get it," she said to the housekeeper.

The girl picked up the phone and looked at the number. She paused, not recognizing it. She was not going to pick up the phone, but then something made her decide to answer it anyway.

Slowly she said, "Hello?"

Trinity sat in her hotel room and could not bring the words out.

"Hello?" the voice on the other end asked again.

Finally, before the girl in Canada could hang up, Trinity spoke. "Hello, uh, Maria or Carl Warner home?"

"Sorry, they are not here now. They are at our summer home. Can I take a message and let them know when they check in?"

Trinity just sat there. She paused, not knowing what to say. Finally the words came to her. The voice on the other end of the phone had been lost to her. It had been fifteen years since she had heard the voice.

"Bianca?" she asked.

"Yes." the girl on the other end said. "Who is this?" There was a pause. "Trinity?"

Trinity froze. "I'm sorry I called. Tell them they…"

Then Trinity hung up the phone. She sat there and started to cry. She lay down on the bed and cried for the next hour.

March 27, 2016

That Sunday, the eight went to church for Communion. They returned to the same church where they had been married. They each took turns asking for forgiveness, and Trinity once again began to cry.

Later that afternoon, they made their way to the Santiago Zoo and wandered around looking at the animals. They were now so desperate to get hold of their new passports that any diversion would help take their minds off the wait.

The children could not understand why anyone would want to keep animals in cages. Bianca felt sorry for them pacing back and forth, trying to find a way out, to be free. Trinity looked at the animals. She felt the same way. Time was running out, and she and the others needed to say their good-byes.

March 29, 2016

Finally good news. They all sat in the office of Klaus and watched as he handed out the eight new passports.

"Here you go. I do not understand what this is all about. But I wish you well and hope you can now go home and find your family," he said.

"Thank you," Jacob said as he shook the man's hand.

Trinity stepped up to Klaus. "Thank you for helping and caring. We owe you a lot for your help."

"Miss Warner, you have no idea what I had to do to make this happen. I may be looking for a new job in the near future. I hope your father is hiring. Good luck," Klaus said.

And with that, they turned and left his office and the building. As they stood on the street in front of the embassy, they looked down at their new passports. Now they were people of the year 2016. Now they could travel, move on, find their loved ones, and, from a distance, say their good-byes. It was now clear that this journey was more about putting their own hearts at rest, being at peace before they would have to move on, being able to say the good-byes none of them were able to do on that March 24 morning.

March 30, 2016

Trinity and Jacob left the bank with a debit card and the knowledge they now had $32,000 dollars to use to cover bills and buy airplane tickets to travel home. They felt good. It was a feeling like the one they had felt in Lisbon when they sold their first diamond in the diamond market of Portugal in 1742. Tonight, as they did on December 13, 1742, they would once again celebrate life with food and drinks. This time, their children would be by their side.

Chapter Nine

Convergence

March 31, 2016

In the waters of the Mediterranean, in the port of Palma de Mallorca, sat a thirty-two-meter yacht. On her stern was the name *Trinity*. This morning, seated for breakfast were Carl and Maria Warner, both in their mid-to-late forties. The ship's crew tended to their needs as they enjoyed their meal.. The day was beautiful; the air was warm, the sky clear.

Next to Carl were his morning paper and his cell phone. As they ate, the phone next to him rang. Carl looked at it and then turned to decline the call.

"Who was that?" Maria asked.

"Don't know. Some DC number," Carl replied.

They sat there a few more seconds, until the phone rang again.

"Just get it," Maria said as she picked up Carl's paper and started to look at it.

Carl answered the phone. "Hello?"

On the other end was a man by the name of Jeff Corral. He was sitting in his car, driving to work in Washington, DC. The time was 6:00 a.m. local for him.

"Hello, who is this?" Jeff asked.

Back on the yacht, Carl leaned forward, somewhat annoyed by the call. "Carl Warner. Who is this?"

The voice on the phone said, "Jeff Corral, I am friends with Marine Colonel Myers. We met two years ago in San Diego."

Carl thought for a minute. "Yes, I think I recall now."

"The reason I am calling is in regards to an e-mail I got this morning from a contact in Germany. She informed me that in the last forty-eight hours, a passport was issued for a Trinity Warner-Kennedy and, on the same day and time, one for a Jacob Conrad Kennedy."

Carl looked to Maria and then turned away from her.

"Are you still there?" Jeff asked.

"Yes, I am. Go ahead." Carl paused. "Could be someone with the same names. Happens."

"That's what I thought since this Trinity is thirty-three years old and has two children."

"Sorry, what did you say?"

"I said thirty-three—"

"No, how many children?"

"Two."

"Two, what are their names?" Carl asked.

In the car, Jeff was looking for the e-mail on the seat next to him. He found it and picked up the phone again. "Bianca and Christopher Kennedy."

Carl replied, "Are you sure?"

"That is what the e-mail listed."

Carl looked back to Maria, who was flipping through the newspaper, paying no attention to him on the phone. "How old are the children?"

"One is thirteen, the other I guess nine," Jeff replied on the phone.

Carl sat there in silent shock.

"Are you still there?"

"Sorry, yes. Do you know where they issued the passports?"

"Santiago, Chile."

Carl leaned forward in the chair. "Interesting, but this woman is way too old to be my daughter. And the fact she has two children, nine and thirteen, there is no way it could be her."

"No, you are right. Just the names matched, and I thought…"

"No, I appreciate the call. Really great how you were thinking of us after all these years. Thank you, Jeff. Really, thank you," Carl said.

"Hey, no problem. We were all hoping it could be her. Take care."

"You too. Bye."

Carl ended the call and placed the phone down on the table. He glanced at Maria.

Maria said, "Good news or bad?"

"Good news. Would you be open to heading to Chile?"

Maria looked at him. "Sure, when?"

"Tonight."

"What? You're kidding?"

"No, I have some business to look at, and I thought you could visit your family there."

"All right. I'll get ready," Maria said as she smiled at her husband and got up from her chair. She walked over and kissed him, then left the back boat deck to prepare for her trip to Chile.

Carl sat there looking at her and then turned to look out at the open water of the bay. "Trinity, could it be you?"

He stood and walked into the main lounge of the yacht. There on the mantel was a photo of Trinity with the family, one of the last photos ever taken of her. Carl smiled.

"Wait for us."

July 2337

The red-robed man sat in a futuristic garden hall in the Gate-keeper temple. In the background, one could still make out the massive

R. C. Richter

graphene computers that ran the length of the main hall, with the central river running down the center.

He was drinking tea, while birds with beautiful blue and yellow colors flew around in the background. Other robed people, men and women, walked about behind him.

A voice came in over an intercom for the red-robed man. "Minister."

The red-robed man placed his tea down. "Yes?"

"We have just detected a new change in the timeline which could affect the outcome of the set mission."

"Send it to me." The red robe pulled from his pocket a clear data pad. He waited a second as the information appeared on the pad. He read it quickly and then looked up, very concerned. "Is Gustavo aware of this?"

"This information was not conveyed to him," the voice said.

The red-robed man stood. "Put me through to Gustavo."

The main gate chamber of the cave was an area untouched by man, an area left, set aside, to cross time. The stone in the hall had been the same for the last ten thousand years. This was where the Gatekeepers would fold, or cross, time. Lab personnel were walking around cleaning up equipment just outside this area.

The red-robed man's voice came in over the intercom. "Gustavo."

A light-green-robed man stopped doing his work and answered the call. "Minister?"

"I need you to *stop* Gustavo and his team before they fold to 2016. He must not go. Tell him the mission is cancelled. We have just detected in the timeline that Trinity and Keara have their children with them! This action can only mean they will be returning to 1755 to maintain the flow, the timeline. For without their children, all that is or ever will be can no longer exist!"

The green-robed man stood there, listening to the minister's concerns. "But, Minister, Gustavo and his team folded eighteen minutes ago. They are gone. They have arrived in the first week of April 2016 as instructed."

Back in the garden, the red-robed man stood. He looked around. What had he done? What had the Gatekeepers done?

He looked up and spoke. "When is the next gate to 2016?"

"The next recorded gate is in six cycles, Minister. If we used the same gate, there is a sixty percent chance that the next team will arrive after Gustavo has left the cave and started this mission," the voice said.

"We have to try!" the red-robed man said.

At the exact same time, in a darkened white marble room filled with candles, KA was in morning prayers. He was on his knees with his eyes closed. Suddenly his eyes snapped open; it was as if KA knew. The fabric of time was in danger of changing. His place in the universe was in danger of ending. The secret of time travel was now in danger of never being discovered. If the children did not return to 1755, they could not pass on Trinity's message, and the circle could not exist anymore.

April 2, 2016

Jacob sat in front of the slate computer, looking at Internet links. His face was tired and strained. "God, I just can't do this anymore."

"Do what?" Trinity asked as she sat on the couch, looking at photos on her iPhone.

"This computer stuff. I used to be so good at it, but now I can't even see the display right."

"You know, you should get new glasses. Now is the time."

Jacob looked at his old, beat-up glasses. "Yes, you're right."

"When am I ever wrong?" Trinity smirked.

Jacob once again looked down at the computer. He then called to Trinity. "Come look at this."

Trinity walked over to Jacob at the desk. There on the display was the Internet page dedicated to the Warner-Kennedy Corp. Trinity got close to the computer so she could see.

Jacob said, "Look in the corner of the screen. See the company logo?" He pointed to a logo, a crest made up of three parts. First, on the left side of the crest, was a North American Native man, on the right side was a sea battle of sailing ships, and on the bottom of the crest was a diamond. "Look familiar?"

"Yes, our crest. Two hundred and seventy-five years and our crest carries on."

"More than just carries on, Trinity. Your family has used the knowledge we left them and are now one of the richest on the planet! Keara and Tom's side is also part of it. Your family is into everything. Your dad and mom are rich, and I mean very rich."

"We changed history?" Trinity asked.

"I don't believe you can change history. I'm not sure how this whole thing played out, but I think your family was always this rich. In the story on the Internet, they talk about how Carl and Maria Warner lost their daughter Trinity in a caving accident. She was lost in the Chungo Caves with her friends on March 24, 2014."

Trinity sat back on the side of the chair. "So?"

"So, Trinity, for any of this that we see here to happen, we had to go back in time. I believe your parents knew this and let you go that day. They let us all go that day. If not, none of this would exist."

"But, we never had this much money?"

"Didn't you? Or so you thought. Your family would have spent every day of your life getting you ready for what was expected of you. If hiding the full value of your worth from you meant you would have a better chance to make it on the other side, they would have done that," Jacob said.

"I wrote in my diary for them not to stop us, for it was the greatest journey of all time."

"And they didn't, Trinity. They respected your wish."

"They knew?"

"They knew, Trinity; they knew the day you were born. They knew what was expected of you. They knew what was expected from all of us. You laid it out for them."

Trinity was at a loss for words. "Holy crap."

"Holy crap. That's the best you can do? That was deep, dear," Jacob joked. "What's wrong?"

"The last fifteen years, I have cried myself to sleep feeling like I let my mother and father down, wanting to say good-bye, and now I found out they knew."

"Trinity, it doesn't change anything. Do you think it was easy for them to let you go that morning? Think about it. You were their daughter, and that cold March morning, they let you walk out of their home for the last time. That would be like letting Bianca walk out of our home knowing you would never see her again. How would that make you feel?"

Trinity started to fight back her tears. "Sad and angry."

"Yes, and that is how I would feel, sad and angry at losing my loving daughter, never to see her again." Jacob turned in his chair and faced Trinity. "We started this as a personal journey to say our good-byes to our families. That includes mine, Trinity. Your mother and father knew. My mom and dad did not know. I left that cold morning under the belief I would return the next day, and I didn't. So for me, I need to say good-bye, Tom needs to say good-bye, and maybe even Keara has to say good-bye. And deep down, even you need to say good-bye."

Trinity tried to wipe the tears from her eyes. "I need to go for a walk; I need to get out of here."

"Can I come with you?"

"No, Jacob, I need to be alone now. It may be the first time ever, but I want to be alone!"

"I understand, Trinity. When you are ready, I will be there. Like I have been there for the last fifteen years."

Trinity took her purse and started to leave the hotel suite just as Bianca and Christopher walked in. They could see she was crying.

"Mamá, what's wrong?" Bianca asked.

Trying to stop crying, Trinity said, "Nothing, dear, nothing. See you all later for dinner." And with that, she left, closing the door behind her.

Bianca and Christopher looked at their father.

"Why is Mother crying?" Christopher asked.

"Your mother just found out there are things which are expected of us in life. She found out we all have a part to play. Some play a much bigger part than others, but at the end, we all have a place in the story of life." Jacob looked at his children. "You have a very large part to play." He paused. "And your mother and I will not always be there to be part of it. You, in time, will have to go it alone. The good news is you do well at playing your part."

As night fell on Santiago, Trinity returned to the suite. Waiting for her were her family—Keara, Tom, the children, and Jacob.

Trinity closed the door behind her. "Sorry, needed some time alone."

"We know," Keara said.

"Are we ready for dinner?" Trinity asked.

Jacob turned to the children. "Can you four please go next door and get ready for dinner?"

The children stood and slowly left the room for next door.

"Trinity, we have something we want to show you," Jacob said.

"More good news?"

"Not quite," Keara said.

"Come here and look at this," Jacob said as he pointed to the computer display. "Come sit down."

Trinity sat down at the desk. "What am I looking at?"

Jacob pointed to the screen. "Here, this is a screenshot taken three hours ago. The computer brought up a message that it detected a second graphene computer on the global network. Right here in the Andaman Sea, Thailand. It was online for twelve minutes, until it went off-line."

Trinity looked at the others, not clear on what was going on.

"Markus told us he crossed over from an island in the Andaman Sea," Jacob said.

Trinity joined in. "You think the Gatekeepers are here?"

"I don't know what to think at this time. But it is something we need to watch and be aware of."

"But how? How would they know we are here in this time?"

"Easy, we are all German citizens now, and that information would have gone into a computer for people in the future to know about. And access."

"Markus said they were looking for him, hunting him because he'd stayed in the past and that was not allowed." Trinity said, as she leaned ahead in the chair.

"And we are in the future, where we no longer belong!" Jacob said.

Keara jumped into the conversation. "Can they track our graphene computer here?"

"Don't know. I don't think so, looks like Markus set this one to detect other graphene computers. Ours is set not to send any information, only pull it in."

"So chances are, they have no way of knowing where we are?" Keara asked.

"Chances are yes, they have no way of knowing," Jacob said.

April 3, 2016

Just after midnight, a twin-engine Gulfstream jet with a crest of a Native, ship, and diamond on its tail, touched down at Santiago International Airport.

The plane taxied to the executive area to deplane its passengers. The Chilean customs agent was on hand. After a quick review of their papers and passports, Maria and Carl stepped from the jet to a waiting white SUV. The SUV left the airport and headed east toward the centre of Santiago, an area known as Las Condes. Thirty minutes later, the SUV pulled up to the Ritz-Carlton. This would be where the Warners would spend the next few days in Santiago as Carl secretly looked for his daughter Trinity.

At lunchtime, the eight time travellers were on the streets of Santiago again. Jacob had just left the optometrist with two new sets of glasses.

"How do I look?" Jacob asked.

"Like a gentleman," Trinity hinted.

From there they departed to see more of the city and sights, and yes, they did stop to eat a *Completo*, a Chilean hot dog loaded with absolutely everything. As they sat in an open-air market eating, they talked about getting ready to leave Santiago and heading north to Canada to make their personal journey of saying good-bye.

Trinity sat there quietly, thinking. She knew most likely her parents would not be in Calgary. Her sister told her that much. Her parents could be travelling anywhere in the world; money was obviously no issue to them. For now her parents would wait. Her friends needed their turn.

At 2:00 p.m., Carl Warner said good-bye to his wife, who was planning to meet one of her relatives for a late tea. He stepped into a cab and headed to the German embassy. Carl thought this was as good as any place to begin the search. After all, they issued the passports, or so he was told.

By two thirty he was in the lobby of the embassy, waiting for Klaus. Klaus met Carl, and the two exchanged handshakes.

"Thank you for seeing me on such short notice," Carl said.

"More than happy to, Mr. Warner."

"I am here in regards to my daughter. I was told that your office issued her a passport?"

Klaus stood there looking at him. "My, you have spies everywhere. Yes, the German government issued her a new passport after she lost her old one."

"Here's the thing. I am looking for my daughter and her friends. We got in late last night, and I was hoping you could tell me where she is."

"Sorry, Mr. Warner, they came to this office three times. The third was to retrieve their passports. We never talked about where they were staying in Santiago."

"No indication of what hotel, a friend's home, anything?"

"No, sorry. Never came up in all the talks we had," Klaus said.

"OK, thank you." Carl was about to turn away, then stopped. "Can you tell me how old she was?"

"Sorry?"

"How old was Trinity?"

"The age she put down was thirty-three. Why?"

"No, just wondering. How were her children?"

"Good, happy. Curious, always looking at things, asking questions between themselves. Very polite, you don't see that anymore."

"Thank you. If, by chance, they once again stop in, can you tell her that her dad is looking for her and we are at the Ritz-Carlton?"

"Happy to."

With that, Carl turned and walked out of the embassy, looking for the next clue. He pulled out his cell phone and made a call to his office in Cologne, Germany.

The phone rang through first to a desk and then on to a cell phone in the home of Erika Karst. Erika, a woman of forty, was one of Carl's overseas assistants who worked for the Warner-Kennedy Corp.

Erika answered her cell phone. "Hello?"

"Erika. Carl here."

"Yes, Carl, the line is very bad; I can hardly make you out."

"Erika, I need you to call all the hotels in Santiago and find out if there is a Trinity Kennedy or Jacob Kennedy staying at any of them."

"All the hotels?"

"Yes, all the hotels."

"That will take time."

"I know. Get help if you need it."

"If I find anything, can I call you back at this number?"

"Yes."

"All right, I'll see what we can do."

Carl ended the call and started to walk toward the main street in hopes of finding a cab.

After dinner, the group once again met in Trinity and Jacob's room.

"Anything in regards to our mystery computer?" Keara asked.

Jacob pulled out the graphene computer and opened it. "Yes, two things."

Trinity turned around in her chair to look at the computer.

"Yesterday, we had a computer found in the Andaman Sea. Then it showed up again here in Dubai after it once again came online in London for three minutes. However, just a few minutes ago, it came online in Tokyo. So, not sure what's up. Like they are not sure where to go next," Jacob said.

Trinity leaned in to look closer. She noticed something no one else had seen. "It's not the same computer."

"What?" Jacob said.

"Look here. The last two numbers at the end of the registration numbers are different. It's a second computer. This one is heading the other way."

Jacob looked closer. "She's right!"

Keara joined in. "We need to book some flights in the morning and move on. If we are going to head north to Calgary, we need to get it done asap. We have passports, and I want to see my parents one last time."

"Keara is right, enough with this. We are here for a reason, so let's move on," Tom said.

"Fine. We can try and book them now, but there is no guarantee there is any room on any of the flights tomorrow."

"Whatever. We get the next one that has room." Keara said.

Jacob started to search for an airline that would take them north.

April 4, 2016

The flights were booked. The eight would be leaving on the seventh, heading north to Toronto and then on to Calgary. By midnight of the eighth, they would once again be home. After fifteen years, they would step foot in the city they left behind that March morning.

This morning, Carl Warner went to the Santiago police looking for their help in finding his daughter. He met with a senior officer at the main police station. They talked about the problem, but he was told they could not help. She was not missing, and being a woman of thirty-three, she was old enough to take care of herself. Carl left empty-handed, flagged down a cab, and headed back to the hotel. In the cab, he once again called Erika.

The phone rang and then picked up. "Erika. Carl. Anything?"

The voice on the other end responded, "No, we are calling, but there are hundreds of hotels, and so far nothing."

Little did Carl and Erika know, but when Trinity put a name down on the registry, she put her last name as Medina-Kennedy, which was her mother's last name and then Jacob's. The problem was the desk clerk put down only the first last name, leaving Kennedy off. Erika had called the Marriott on the first day, but asked for Warner or Kennedy, not Medina. They had overlooked the obvious. They were now within blocks of each other, but still worlds apart.

At noon, the group met to head out for lunch. Jacob updated them that one graphene computer was in Toronto and the other in Vancouver.

Trinity sat with the others, looking at the information being presented to them from Jacob. "Bet you the next time we see those computers come online, they will be in Santiago," she said.

"One bet I am not going to take," Keara said.

"I thought you said they cannot track us or this computer?" Trinity asked.

"I must be wrong."

"Then turn it off," Keara said.

"I don't think it has an off."

"It must. They can turn theirs off. We see them; then we don't."

"We have to leave it on. We need to know when they get here so we can move before they find us," Trinity said.

"I agree," Jacob added.

"Fine, whatever. The whole thing freaks me out. The last thing I want is to put our children in danger."

Keara looked at her friends. "Let's eat, may be the last good meal we have before we move on."

Noon passed, night came, and Jacob kept an eye on the computer, but nothing. No more signs. Just after midnight, he turned in after looking in on his two children to make sure they were safe.

He lay next to Trinity in bed. "Good night, dear, love you." He kissed her as he had done for the last fifteen years.

Two more days and they would be leaving Santiago for the last time and heading north. From there it was anyone's guess. The only thing they needed to do was head to Playa del Carmen. There they would find a set of caves that would once again return them to the past, and a waiting ship, a past that was now their real home. Being in the present was fun for the first few days, but now the world was starting to close in on them. Trinity was now starting to second-guess her wish. Some things were better left alone.

"Good night, Jacob," Trinity said.

April 5, 2015

They started to pack. Trinity looked at all the stuff she already had collected. She knew she could not take any of these beautiful items along. There was no way she could carry any of it. She could take only what would be key in life and the coming few years ahead. For her it would be her iPhone, and cases, to protect the message and photos it carried within it. She once again looked at the phone. It would have to return to the past only for it to be passed down nine generations to one day return to this time.

We all have a part to play, she thought.

Jacob walked in with a large plastic travel case he would use to pack the three field gate generators. "Excuse me," he said as he pushed his way through the room.

In just over twenty-four hours, they would be boarding an airplane and flying north to Canada. In Canada, it would be spring. In Chile, it was fall now, and the first of the leaves were turning golden yellow.

Trinity looked out the window at the streets below. She thought that perhaps she should have searched out other family here in Santiago. But, her goal would still be to find her mother and father before they returned to the past.

That night, Carl returned to his hotel room to meet his wife, Maria, for dinner. He was tired and beat after the long day. Again he had had no luck finding his daughter or her friends. Little did he know, he was within ten blocks of the hotel she was staying at.

"How was your day? Did you get your business done?" Maria asked him.

"No, not yet. Still working at it. I hope tomorrow."

April 7, 2016

This morning, Maria said good-bye to Carl as he once again headed out for his secret search. Maria was going shopping at the mall Parque Arauco, which was just down the street from the Marriott Hotel.

Maria left the hotel room and walked toward the elevators, purse in hand.

Meanwhile, Trinity and the others were finishing their packing. The time was just after nine thirty. Jacob closed the lid on the plastic trunk, which now held the three field gates safely within.

"The flight is at seven forty, and we have lots of time. I want to take the kids shopping one last time for a few more things they will need over the next few weeks," Trinity said.

"All right, but please nothing they can't carry or, more importantly, shouldn't take back. The last thing I want them to do is get too attached to something from this time and then have it taken away from them. Just not fair." Jacob said.

"I know."

Keara, Tom, and the four children entered the second suite to see how things were going.

"Are we leaving?" asked Bianca.

"Yes, head on down. Just finishing some stuff. Meet you all down there," Trinity said.

"OK, everyone out," Keara said to Tom and the children. "See you downstairs. We'll get two cabs."

"Sounds good. I think Jacob is going to stay here."

Jacob looked up. "Yes. Make sure you are back by one."

Keara, Tom, and the children headed out. Trinity worked at finishing packing. She once again looked at all the stuff and thought, what was she thinking?

The cab with Maria inside was now a few blocks from the mall, stuck in traffic. She looked out the window and saw the first of the leaves fall from the trees lining the streets. She thought back to the years she lived in Santiago, how much she liked it here.

Tom, Keara, and the children stepped into the elevator. As they did, they passed a cleaning cart being pushed by a man dressed in a white housekeeper uniform.

Back in the room, Trinity dropped her last bag on the floor. "There, see you at one."

"Great. Love you. Be safe," Jacob said to her.

Trinity stepped from the suite into the hall and walked past the man and his cart, toward the elevators.

Jacob sat down at the desk, opened the lid on the graphene computer, and logged in. The computer came to life. "Let us see where our two visitors are this morning," Jacob said to himself.

He sat there waiting for the system to log in to the web.

In the hall, Trinity made her way to the elevator and pressed the button to head down and meet the others. As she did, a European-looking woman with blonde hair walked around the corner and stood next to her. Trinity could not help but look at this woman. In the last ten years, living and travelling in the Canary Islands and Lisbon, she had seen only dark-haired people. Amsterdam was the last time she saw people with blonde hair. Trinity smiled at her, and she smiled back. The woman was wearing a dark grey suit and dark sunglasses. Trinity was wearing white, her favourite color.

In the room, Jacob stood up to get a cup of coffee. He then returned to the computer. There on the screen was an update showing the last locations of one of the two other graphene computers. The last time he saw, the location was in Toronto, Canada. This time it took him a minute to work out the location.

"What the hell?" He looked closer. The new location was in Santiago, but more than Santiago, it was within a hundred metres of the hotel they were in.

Jacob picked up his cell phone and quickly dialed Trinity's number.

At that instant, Trinity stepped into the elevator with the woman, and the doors closed.

Back in the room, Jacob got a message saying the person was out of network range. "Goddamn it! No! What the hell? She just walked out."

Jacob started to walk toward the door of the suite. As he did, he hit redial on the phone. No luck. He then started to send a text message. It read: *Danger, they are here!*

In the elevator, the two women started to head down from the twenty-fifth floor of the hotel to the main lobby. On the twenty-third floor, the doors to the elevator opened, and on stepped an old woman and a young boy around ten years old. They hit the button to the eighteenth floor. The woman looked over to Trinity and then to the two others in the elevator. The elevator moved down to the eighteenth floor, and the doors opened. The old woman and child stepped off. As they left, Trinity heard the sound of her iPhone in her purse. The doors closed, and as they did, she pulled the phone out and saw the text on the main screen.

Jacob opened the door to the suite to run after Trinity to warn her. As he did, standing in the hall facing him was the man with the housekeeping cart. Their eyes met, and then Jacob looked down at the man's hand. In it he was holding what looked like a futuristic needle injection unit. Jacob looked up just as the man jumped forward and lunged at him. Jacob blocked his move with his phone and pushed away his arm with the needle in it. The two men fell back onto the floor and started to struggle and fight. Jacob managed to knock the needle from his hand, and it went flying under the couch. He rolled over and started to stand to run, but the man then pulled a knife on him and dove at Jacob, pushing him into the bathroom. There the two battled for life and death. The man pushed Jacob to the floor and tried to push the knife into his face, but Jacob's will to live was too strong.

Jacob pushed the knife away with all his strength and then, with his left hand, was able to grab hold of the inner plastic shower curtain and pull it down over the two of them. He then grabbed it with his right hand and pulled the plastic curtain over the head of his attacker. The man started to struggle under the plastic sheet. Jacob managed to spin the man around. Now behind man, Jacob pulled the curtain tighter around his neck and held it. The man struggled, looking for the knife, which was now beside him on the bathroom floor. Jacob saw the knife and then kicked it away.

"Not today, shithead. My day to die is still a few years off!" Jacob said.

The man did all he could, but Jacob wouldn't let him go. Finally the man was overcome due to the lack of oxygen. He quit struggling and slowly dropped limp. Jacob continued to hold him, making sure the man was unconscious or dead.

Finally Jacob dropped his grip and pushed himself away from the body now lying on the bathroom floor. He looked around and noticed blood; the man had somehow cut Jacob on his chest. Jacob looked at it and then grabbed a small towel and placed it over the wound. He then looked for his phone. He stepped into the main suite and, finding it, he picked it up and started to run into the hall, toward the elevator. One elevator was on the ground floor; the other was just passing the tenth floor and heading to the lobby. Jacob started to run toward the stairwell and dialed the number to Keara and Tom. In the stairwell, Jacob charged down the long set of stairs descending to the main floor. As he did, he would from time to time look down the centre shaft to see how much farther he still had to go.

Outside, in front of the hotel, Keara, Tom, and the children were waiting. Two cabs had pulled up just as Keara's cell phone rang in her pocket. She pulled it out.

"Hello, Jacob, change your mind?" Keara asked.

Jacob, running down the stairs, snapped at her over the phone, "Get off the street, back into the hotel lobby; they are trying to kill us!" he screamed.

"What?"

"Damn it, get yourself and the children off the street!"

Keara turned to Tom and started to walk toward him, just as a gunshot rang out and narrowly missed her. The bullet zipped by and broke the pane of glass behind her, smashing it to the ground. Keara turned and then fell to the ground.

Tom looked around and then ducked down just as more gunshots rang out. More glass went flying.

"Keara, stay down!" Tom yelled.

The children looked in shock as this was going on.

Keara screamed at them. "For God's sake, get down behind the cab!"

The children fell to the ground behind the taxicab just as a side window was shot out, sending glass flying over the children.

Men and women on the sidewalk in front of the hotel started to scream.

"*Abajo!*" men screamed in Spanish to the bystanders. "*Abajo!*"

Jacob could hear the shots over the cell phone. "Keara!" he yelled. He then dropped the cell phone and continued to run down the stairs. He passed the tenth floor on his way to the main floor.

Finally he hit the lobby, crashing to the floor as he left the stairwell. From the floor he looked up at the elevator and saw it had now stopped on the third floor. He backtracked and ran up the stairs to the third floor. Out of breath, he struggled to pull the door open from the stairwell. As he stepped into the hall, he saw the elevator doors open. He slowly walked forward, looking for the worst. As he approached, he could see the feet of a woman lying on the floor sticking out from the elevator. The elevator doors were trying to close, but couldn't. He slowed and then looked into the elevator. The first thing he saw was smashed mirror glass; the mirrors in the elevator, above the handrail, were all smashed and cracked. Blood was everywhere. He then stopped and looked down at the elevator floor.

There, sitting on the floor, was Trinity, her back up against the wall panel with the controls on it. She was covered in blood, but very much alive. The European woman was next to her, unconscious. She, too, was covered in blood. Between the two was a futuristic needle like the one the other man had tried to use on him.

Jacob was shocked at the sight. He looked down at Trinity, who looked up at him. "The bitch tried to stick me with that!" she screamed.

Jacob fell to his knees next to Trinity. "Are you OK?"

"I think so; I have a few cuts from the glass."

"Can you stand and walk?"

"Yes, I think so," Trinity said as she tried to stand.

Trinity stepped from the elevator just as the sound of police cars coming down the street could be heard.

"Come on," Jacob said to her as he helped her from the elevator. "Where is your phone?"

Trinity turned and saw it on the floor of the elevator. "There!" She pointed. Jacob reached down and picked it up and started to dial Keara.

Out in front of the hotel, Keara's phone on the sidewalk started to ring. She reached for it and answered it. "Hello?"

"Are you all right?" Jacob asked.

Keara looked around. "I think so."

"What happened?"

"I don't know…gunshots. Someone tried to shoot us."

"Are you all right?" Jacob asked again.

"Yes, fine, just scared. The shooter took off. The police are coming."

Back on the third floor, Trinity and Jacob walked to the other elevator and waited to hit the button.

"I hear them. Can you get the children and get back into the hotel and up to our room?" Jacob asked.

Down at the street, Keara looked to Tom. "Yes, on our way." She moved to the cab and the children. "Quickly, get up and run back into the hotel, to the elevator!"

The children did as they were told. They ran into the lobby, toward the elevators. Behind them were Keara and Tom. Tom hit the button.

Keara yelled into the phone, "On our way!"

Jacob hit the button on their floor to head up to the twenty-fifth floor. They waited, and when the doors opened, there standing in the elevator car were Keara, Tom, and the children.

Keara was shocked to see Trinity. "Oh my God, what happened to you?"

Jacob and Trinity stepped into the car. "It can wait. Hit the 'close door' button," Jacob said.

The elevator doors closed, and the car started up. Bianca and Christopher looked at their parents. Both were bleeding.

"Are you all right?" Bianca cried.

"Yes, I'm fine," Trinity said.

A minute later, the elevator stopped on the twenty-fifth floor. The doors opened, and in the hall, the housekeeping cart of the man who had tried to kill Jacob was still there.

The eight entered the suite, and Bianca screamed seeing the dead man in the bathroom.

"Holy crap!" Keara said to Jacob. "What the hell!"

Jacob turned to Tom. "Tom, give me a hand."

Tom paused, trying to get a grasp of what was going on. Then he moved forward to help Jacob. The two men picked up the body of the dead man and started to carry it out.

"Oh man, he peed himself," Tom said.

"That's not all he did. Get the door."

They took the body down the hall and dropped it into the house-keeping cart and covered it with sheets. Then they rolled it down to the far end of the hall and left it.

They returned to the suite and closed the door.

"Now what?" Trinity asked.

"Now we need to clean this mess up. Tom, go get your outer shower curtain and hang it in our bathroom. Keara, we need to clean this blood up," Jacob said.

Jacob looked to Trinity. "We need to get out of this hotel, now, before they find the bodies. If they do, we are stuck here."

Jacob started to pull his shirt off and examine his wound. "How is it?" he asked Trinity.

"Not too bad. Not that deep," Trinity replied.

"Any bandages?"

"No."

Keara walked in. "Here, put a pad on it." She handed him a feminine hygiene pad. "Just place it over it for now, to stop the bleeding. We can hold it in place using some packing tape."

Jacob looked at it uncomfortably and did just that.

Trinity washed her face and tried to clean the cuts and wash off the bloodstains. Tom looked down from the window at the street below. He could see seven police cars now parked in front of the hotel.

"Not good. We need to move before they start searching too hard," Tom suggested.

Ten minutes later, they were ready to move.

The eight left the room, closing the door behind them. Each had one small bag with them, and Jacob had the plastic case with the gates inside. In his shoulder bag he had the computer, passports, plane tickets, gold, and diamonds.

As they got to the elevator, they could see the one was still sitting on the third floor.

Tom turned to Jacob. "Stairs?"

"No!"

"Fine." Tom pressed the button.

They waited, and finally the car came. The doors opened, and they stepped in.

"Where to?" Tom asked.

"Sixth floor, then we stair it to the second and head out through the convention hall," Jacob said.

The doors closed, and the eight descended down to an uncertain outcome.

Chapter Ten

Run

Seated in the backseat of the cab was Maria, going through e-mails on her phone. The cab driver signaled to get off the President Kennedy expressway, onto the side road heading east, which would pass by the Parque Arauco mall. The cab slowed down to let Maria out. But, as they got closer, they could see police everywhere. The mall, like all the other buildings, was being evacuated due to the shooting. The cab moved back into traffic and started to speed up.

"¿Qué está pasando? Maria asked what was going on.

The cab driver replied he was not sure, but the police were not letting him stop. He would have to drop her off somewhere else.

Maria leaned forward and looked out the side window at the police presence. As the cab picked up speed, she looked over at the Marriot Hotel and saw all the yellow police tape being pulled out around the building.

Then, for reasons that will never be known, she looked into the crowd of people on the street. In the crowd were eight people pulling or carrying suitcases. Maria looked at them, thinking how strange, and then looked closer. Her mind pulled her eyes to the woman and man in the lead; these were two faces she had seen every day for the first thirty years of her life. They were the faces that hung over the fireplace in the main study of the La Palma estate home she lived in.

"Trinity, Jacob!" Maria said.

Then, as quick as she had set eyes on them, they once again disappeared in the crowd. She turned her head and tried to look out the back of the cab to where they were.

"*Pare!*" she screamed, telling the driver to stop.

The driver said he couldn't, not here. She snapped at him to stop as she started to open the door of the moving car. The driver stepped on the brakes so fast that the car behind them almost hit them.

Maria ran from the cab, down the middle of the road, around the cars, looking for the eight. But, they had melded into the crowd and were gone. She desperately started to run between people, hoping to spot the faces again, but to no avail. She called out the names of Trinity and Jacob, hoping they would hear her.

Maria was left standing in the crowd, lost. She turned around and around, but no Trinity or Jacob. Standing on the sidewalk, Maria pulled out her phone and dialed Carl's number.

Carl, who was just sitting down with a private investigator, answered the call. "Sí."

"Carl, I think I just saw Trinity and Jacob," Maria said.

Carl's jaw dropped. He could not believe her words. "Where?" he yelled.

"In front of the Marriott Hotel."

"Just now?" Carl asked.

"Yes, a few seconds ago, but I lost them in the crowd, and I can't see them anymore."

"Are you sure?"

"I think so, but how?"

"Keep looking for them. I'm on my way."

"What do you mean? Did you know they were here?"

"No time, keep looking for them. I will call you when I get close."

Maria ended the call and dropped the phone to her side. She looked at all the people walking toward and away from her. She started to walk up the street in the same direction they were walking. She walked faster, and as she did, she started to cry out Trinity's name.

Two cabs pulled up in front of the Santiago Airport departures area. Out stepped the eight time travellers, with their few bags and case. Jacob paid the two cabs, and then the group walked into the airport terminal.

They made their way to the Air Canada counter to check in. They were a few hours early, but the ticket woman still took them. She looked at each of the passports and then issued the boarding passes.

They left the ticket counter and headed upstairs to the restaurant to wait until they could head through customs and on to the gate. In the restaurant, they sat down to catch their breath.

The children looked scared, lost and bewildered. Trinity looked at her children and then at Keara's.

"Are you all right?" she asked.

They all looked at her, and Bianca started to cry. Trinity leaned forward to hold her and give her some comfort.

Jacob sat there looking at the group. Then Keara spoke up. "How did they know we were at that hotel? How did they know we were in Santiago? They made their way straight for us, right from Burma."

Jacob looked at her and the others. "Our passport, hotel records, bank cards, cell phone use? I think all those things are on file in some master computer, and that information survived for the next three hundred–plus years. The Gatekeepers were able to access it and follow the trail right to us."

They all looked at Jacob. "Oh shit," Keara said. "We're screwed then. They'll know we are on this flight and that we are heading to Calgary."

"They will," Jacob added.

"What are we going to do?" Trinity asked.

"We can't go home anymore. What's to say they won't be waiting for us?" Keara said.

"She's right. They want us dead because we stepped out of our time," Tom said.

"Yes, but unless we get our children back, there will be no future for us or the Gatekeepers." Jacob looked at the children. "They're the ones who carry the message forward to their children and so on. Right up to the point Markus talked about, when science starts to take an interest."

"We can't go to Calgary anymore," Keara pointed out.

"But what about what we planned to do?" Trinity asked.

Keara looked at her.

Jacob pulled his bag up, took out a writing pad, tore some sheets of paper from it, and placed them in front of each of the four.

Keara asked, "What is this?"

Jacob replied, "Your message to your parents. Your good-bye." He then pulled out a pencil and two pens.

Tom, Keara, and Trinity looked at each other. Slowly they each started to write. Jacob went to the counter to ask for a spare pen he could use.

When he returned, he sat down just as Keara stopped and rolled the paper into a ball. "No, not doing it. I came on this trip to make my own peace. I came to say my own good-bye before I die. To look at them one last time from across a park or mall or something. Leaving them a message like this will only bring back all the pain again for them." Keara looked to Trinity and smiled. "Markus told us your message made it. Our parents knew what became of us, the journey we lived." She looked to her children. "The wonderful children we gave birth to. The home we built, the wonderful men we married. The life we had. No need to bring pain back into their lives. It is better that they remember us as we were. To them, we are dead and gone, and that is how it should be."

Trinity looked at Keara. She then looked down at the paper and also rolled it into a ball. The children just sat there staring at their parents.

"We can't go to Calgary," Keara said again.

"I know," Jacob replied. "We won't, but we still need to go to Toronto. From there we will get a flight to Mexico and wait until the gate is ready for us to cross six weeks from now."

Bianca asked, "What's happening?"

Trinity turned to her daughter. "Your mother made a mistake. She wanted so badly to say good-bye to her mother and father that she forgot that her children are more important. She forgot how important they are and what is expected of her children in the coming years."

"Mamá, you didn't make a mistake. You showed us who and what we are, who our parents are, and almost who our grandparents were."

Trinity looked at her children. "You would have loved my mom and dad. They were so kind and loving; I wish I could have shown them to you." She smiled as she fought back tears.

"Someday you still may. After all, we are time travellers."

"That we are," Trinity said. "That we are."

At six thirty, the eight made their way to the departure hall and customs. They showed their passports to the customs official, who asked for their immigration cards, which they never had from the start. Jacob told them how they had lost all their papers when they were stolen, and just the other day they had gotten new passports. The agent asked them to fill in some forms and then they could be on their way.

Fifteen minutes later, they sat at the gate, waiting for their flight north. No one felt like talking anymore. Deep down they felt beaten. Their hope of saying good-bye in their own way was now gone. Perhaps Keara was right. It was better to finally let it go, remember them as they were, as their parents would remember them, the children who never came home.

At 8:10, the plane finally took off from Santiago International Airport and headed north. Trinity looked one last time down at the city that she considered her second home, a city that once again had welcomed her and the others back into the twenty-first century. Slowly the city lights faded from view. Like so much of life's journey, this would just be one more stop along the way before Trinity and the others would depart this world for the last time.

Sitting in a cab heading back to the Ritz-Carlton, Maria and Carl were silent. Maria just gazed out the cab window at the city lights.

"Are you going to say anything?" Carl asked.

Maria continued to look out the window. "You knew. Yet you didn't tell me."

"No, because I was not sure. It was a rumor, and if I was wrong, I didn't want to break your heart. We lost her once, and I was not going to bring you more pain."

"If I would have known, I would have been looking for her."

"If you would have known, chances are you wouldn't have ever gone to the mall today."

"What now?"

"What now, indeed. We keep searching. She and the others are alive and well somewhere in Santiago. We keep searching until we no longer can." Carl said.

Maria turned and looked at him. Little did they know that night that Trinity and the others had left Santiago and were now en route for Toronto, Canada.

Just after midnight, Gustavo, dressed as a Carabinero, a Chilean police officer, walked into a police station at▢ 17 Avda Las Tranqueras.

This station was only a few kilometres from where the shooting took place. Gustavo easily walked past the other police officers, as they were busy at their desks dealing with the events of the day. Events like what had unfolded on this day didn't happen in Santiago, so everyone was on edge.

Gustavo, who stood six feet tall, made his way through the front security area and into the back offices. From there he walked down a long hall, which led to a group of jail cells. Two officers walked past him, giving him little attention. As he made his way down the center of the jail cells, he looked at each of them. They were filled with a number of people who had been arrested over the course of the day. As he approached the end of the cells, he stopped in front of a cell occupied with three women. One of the women was the European from the elevator who Trinity had battled earlier that day.

The woman sat there looking at the floor. She had a number of small bandages that covered up the marks from the fight. Her face was bruised from where Trinity had hit her.

Gustavo turned and stood at the jail bars, looking at her. The woman first saw the boots of a man, and then she slowly gazed up at him. She wiped the hair from her face to get a better view. She looked at Gustavo, who in turn looked down at her. Their eyes met. She leaned her head to one side and smiled at him.

Gustavo hesitated for a moment as he looked at her. He then pulled his side arm from his holster, a Glock pistol, and pointed it at her. She just kept looking at him, then smiled and closed her eyes. Gustavo fired the gun, striking the woman in the head, killing her instantly. The other women in the cell started to scream and panic.

As the women screamed, other Chilean officers started to run down the long hall toward Gustavo. He then turned the gun on himself, held it to his head, and pulled the trigger.

His body dropped to the floor just as two officers ran up to him, shouting, "*Pare!*"

August 2337

KA sat at his desk quietly, looking at a number of clear display pads in front of him. As he did, the red-robed man entered and walked to his desk. There he stood for the longest time, waiting for KA to acknowledge his presence.

Finally KA looked up at him.

"KA, we have once again seen a change in the timeline knowledge as it is and as it was recorded. A man and woman were killed at a police station in Santiago, Chile. Neither had any names or ID on them. We believe they were two members of the team sent to end the lives of the Origins."

KA looked at the man. "Has the team returned yet?"

"No, the next window is in four more cycles," the red-robe man said.

"Any news on the Origins?"

"No, KA. The last we know from historical records is they boarded a flight from Santiago to the city of Old Toronto."

"There are no other recorded changes in the timeline?" KA asked.

"No. These are the only ones at this time. The system continues to cross-check from what is known history to what is now evolving on a day-to-day basis."

KA sat back in his chair. "The children of Trinity and Keara are still in the timeline from 1755 and on?"

"Yes, just as they should be."

"Then let us hope Gustavo has the wisdom to come home, before any more lives are lost. Given time, and the right clues along the way, we will once again go after the Origins, but this time, free of their children." KA looked at the man. "You can go now."

With that, KA went back to his work.

April 8, 2016

The Air Canada flight touched down at the Toronto International Airport. The eight time travellers started to deplane. Bianca, Erich, and the other children looked wide-eyed, lost; in the last few weeks, so much had happened to them. One day they were living in 1754, and the next day they were in 2016 and had found out their parents were time travellers. For any child this would have been an overwhelming event. But add in the historical differences, and you could see why the four children were acting this way. But still, Trinity and Keara were very proud of them. They were handling it like veterans.

After they left the aircraft, the first thing Jacob and Tom did was to go to the ticket desk and see about changing their flights to Mexico. Trinity and Keara sat quietly with their children, waiting. Trinity looked at the four children. The sights and sounds were overwhelming for them.

"How you doing?" Trinity asked Bianca.

"I want to go home," she said.

"I know, soon now. Soon you will be in your room next to the sea, watching the waves roll in."

Just then, Jacob and Tom returned. "OK, we have a flight at twelve forty-five today to Cancún. From there we will have to head south and find a place to hide until we have to go to the cave for the crossover, which will be six weeks from now."

"Will they come after us?" Keara asked.

"I don't know. Yes, maybe. That is why the second we land, we have to start using different names at the places we end up staying at. Then when the time is right, we will head to Playa del Carmen and to the caves there for the crossing."

It was then that I started to question all the things we had done. Perhaps I should have let go of my parents, but for fifteen years, it was my dream to see them one last time, to know they were OK without me. I never did see them, but the legacy they left around the world proved to me that they were fine without me. I also had the chance for the last time to hear the voice of my younger sister, Bianca. Perhaps as Keara said, some things are better left alone. We would now move on to Mexico and spend the next six weeks hiding from those who would try to kill us. For history to play out as it should, we would have to make sure our children returned to the past.

I looked at my family and the family of Keara and Tom. We had done well. I just hoped that once they returned to the past, the children would be happy there. When you give someone the apple from the tree of the Garden of Eden, it is sometimes hard to go back to the way it was. Our children had taken their first bite from the apple, and now they knew what the future held. Use it wisely, my children.

Chapter Eleven

Mexico

May 11, 2016

The eight had found a place to rent for the time they would be in Mexico, at a place called Puerto Maya. It was a small two-story, three-bedroom flat-roof home in a small gated community a five-minute drive to the ocean. Not much to look at, and a far cry from what they were accustomed to, but the owner took cash and asked no questions as to who they were or why they were staying. Most likely the owner thought they were there for the spring to enjoy the beach.

Each day was very much the same. They would sleep in, have breakfast, and then head down to the beach. The sand was white and powdery soft, unlike the coarse black sand of La Palma. The children were starting to make friends, which was a double-edged sword. These were friends they would never see again. Trinity felt bad for them. They were happy, and soon, they would once again be pulled back to their own time—no TV, no radio, nothing that they took for granted each day.

By night, they would most often have dinner at one of the resorts along the coast. The nights were warm, the sky clear this time of the year. On this night, a cruise ship sailed by them. The children were amazed at the size of the ship. The lights made it magical.

Trinity and the others wished they could have shown their children all the things that make the twenty-first century so grand. But, that wouldn't be in the cards. It would be just too unfair to them. They would have to go back to a very simple life, but for them, it would be a life of privilege. This would lessen the blow when the time came.

In just over two weeks, they would once again be stepping across the Rubicon. Their children would not be returning ever again.

May 14, 2016

Saturday, and shopping for one of the last times. What do you get a person from 1754? Before Trinity was born, there was a joke going around. What do you get a Russian for Christmas? Toilet paper, because he doesn't have anything. This of course, was prior to the fall of Communism. This was how Trinity and the others felt. They knew they should return only with what they left with, but how could they? They decided to stock up on some much-needed key items.

Anyone who would have watched them shop that day would have questioned what they saw. Trinity and Keara bought sixty-four toothbrushes, dental floss, twenty tubes of toothpaste, an assortment of medication, creams, and gels, enough to last them for the next four to five years. Trinity and Keara knew their years ahead were short now, but at least their children would have it better than they had for the last fifteen years. The little things like a cream to help with a cut could save the life of a person. If their children planned it right, they could stretch it out a few more years after they were gone. After that, they were once again on their own, living their lives as they did when they were first born into an ancient world some thirteen years ago.

Were the things they were doing right? Who knows, but at the time, it made sense, and anything to make life a little easier was welcomed by all.

They pushed the shopping cart to the till and paid cash for all the items they had. The woman working the till asked if the end of the world was coming. Trinity and Keara looked at each other and then laughed.

Keara said in Spanish, "Just going on a very long trip."

The woman looked at her funny and handed them their change.

That night, they all walked the beach as darkness fell. Trinity held Jacob's hand, her loving husband, as the waves washed in.

"You know what I miss most staying here these last five weeks?" Trinity said.

Jacob stopped and looked at her. "Sunsets."

"How did you know?"

"How could I not? They are the one thing at the end of each day that brings you happiness and fulfilment. I know it because, back home, if, for whatever reason, the sunset is lost because of clouds or a storm, your day is incomplete. It is like your whole day was wasted. Sunsets are the one thing that gives you eternal happiness." Jacob turned and took her other hand and looked into her eyes. "Soon we will be home again, and you will see your sunsets."

Trinity looked at him. "Do you believe there are sunsets in heaven?"

Jacob looked at her. "You asked me this one already."

Trinity waited for an answer from Jacob.

He finally responded, "I hope so."

Perhaps in heaven there are no sunsets, perhaps in heaven there are a lot of things we take for granted each day here on Earth. Perhaps this is why, after a time of rest, we return to Earth to live again. This was what I believed, and as the days came closer to the end, I hoped that God would one day let me return to Earth, with Jacob by my side, so that I could once again feel the sea air and watch the sunsets again.

May 22, 2016

On this day, Jacob and Trinity started out for their first day of reconnaissance of the set of caves they would have to use to return to 1755.

The caves were just outside Playa del Carmen, Mexico, inland at a place called the Secret River, a set of underwater caves that stretched the length of the coast. Trinity and Jacob headed north on Highway 307, driving a borrowed car from the same owner who had rented them the house. They came to a turnoff that took them inland. As they got closer, following the latitude, longitude coordinates provided on the graphene slate computer, they started to realize that the caves in question were not an out-of-the-way place, but in fact were a tourist destination. They turned off a dusty road and came to an area called the Secret Caves.

They pulled into the parking area, where a man came out asking why they had driven their own car. Only small tour buses were allowed, he said. Jacob slowly closed the lid to the computer and stepped out of the car. They apologised to the man and said they didn't know. The man said they would have to book a tour if they wanted to go on the caving adventure.

Trinity and Jacob looked at each other. "You have to be kidding," Jacob said.

"Of all the places we could pick, we end up picking a set of caves which are used daily. This is a joke, right?" Trinity added.

Jacob started to walk toward the main office. "No joke, dear."

"How the hell are we going to make this work?" Trinity asked. "Like really, Jacob, come on. Hi, we want to live in your set of caves for the next six days. I hope you don't mind? Holy cow!"

"Can you take a chill pill! Let me think."

"Think, Jacob. In less than four days, we have to step into that cave!" Trinity snapped at him.

"Really? Thank you for that." Jacob walked away to the office, where for the next ten minutes, they were told about the caves and the history behind them. Jacob asked how far they stretched toward the sea. He was told they went for over twenty kilometres. Jacob asked if he and Trinity could look around. The woman behind the desk told them yes, but they could not leave the trails.

For the next hour, the two walked, searching for the precise location where, below them, under the ground, the cave would allow for a window to open and let them cross.

Finally they came to the spot.

"OK, here. Right below us," Jacob said.

"Here? How does 'here' line up with the cave below?" Trinity asked. "Unless we get a guide, we are SOL."

The two returned to the office and asked if they could get a tour today. The woman behind the counter told them that all tours were booked and they should book at any number of the hotels in the area. Jacob said they were here now and would pay for their private tour. He pulled out US$1,000 dollars and placed it on the desk. The woman looked at it in shock and immediately called the manager. The manager said this was very unusual, but for them, they would make an exception. The problem was there was no photographer to take photos of them in the caves. Jacob said no problem, they were not interested in the photos.

Forty-five minutes later, they were in their wet suits and started out on the tour. The guide's name was Manuel, a man they found out was twenty-two years old and had been doing tours of the caves for three years now.

They started out and walked the jungle trail to the cave entrance. They entered and were soon plunged into darkness. They turned on the head lamps. What they saw from that moment on was unbelievably breathtaking.

The caves went off in all directions. Jacob asked if they were well mapped. Manuel pointed out that they were, but the routes picked were best for the tour groups.

Trinity asked, "So you ever spend a night in the caves?"

"Sí, over the years, I have slept here one or two nights. There are some areas that are out of the water and others totally underwater year round."

"What's it like?" Trinity asked.

"Quiet. Surreal. There are no sounds but for the odd time you hear water dripping," Manuel told them.

For the next hour and a half, they took the tour and then finally returned to the world above. Trinity asked if Jacob knew where the location was that they needed to find underground. He told her that the caves were well mapped on the computer, and now that he knew how to get in, they should be able to find the precise location.

The problem remained how to get in and then stay there for up to six days.

After cleaning up, Trinity and Jacob met Manuel for a glass of Tequila next to an open-air sitting area. Manuel said that normally they had lunch at the end of a tour, but it was just too late in the day.

"We didn't come for the food." Jacob said.

The three continued to talk for the next half hour, about where Manuel was from and what he was studying in school. Trinity asked him if he would have dinner with them tonight in Playa del Carmen. It would be their treat, and they would pay him to show them all the sights of the seaside town.

After some hesitation, he finally said yes. After all, they seemed like nice people.

Jacob picked up his Mexican cell phone and reported back to Keara and Tom on what was going on and that they would not be back until very late.

That night, the three once again met for dinner at a seaside restaurant Manuel had recommended. They laughed about a number of things, and each shared their stories of the interesting places they had visited over the years. Trinity told Manuel about their home on La Palma and how they had a home next to the sea. Manuel said "It must be very nice."

Trinity said, "It truly is a place of beauty, and I look forward to seeing it again."

Finally, by night's end, as they sat by a seaside bar, Trinity asked the million-dollar question. She pulled out an envelope, and from it she dumped a diamond onto the counter.

Manuel looked down at it and said, "What is this?"

"This is yours if you help us. That diamond in front of you has a value of thirty thousand dollars US."

Manuel looked at the both of them. "How can I help you? I don't want anything to do with drugs."

"No, nothing like that. All we want is to spend six days in the cave, all alone, with some friends and our children. We will bring the needed equipment and food, but no one can know we are there, and we need to be left alone!"

Manuel looked at the stone. "How do I know the stone is real?"

Jacob picked up a heavy beer glass and smashed it down on the diamond. The diamond was driven into the wood countertop, and there was not a mark on it.

"There you go," Jacob said.

"That is all you want, to spend six days in the cave?"

"Sí, Manuel. That is all we want. To be left alone off a side tunnel at this location." Trinity pointed to a hand-drawn map. "Don't worry, we wouldn't damage any part of the cave, and once we are gone, you will never know we were ever there."

"When?"

"Five days from now, starting the night of May twenty-eighth. We will have all the equipment we need for our stay. You take us in, and then you leave us. Then, after six days, you come for us, and we leave."

Manuel looked at Trinity and Jacob, and then looked down at the diamond. He was about to speak, when Trinity said, "Thirty thousand dollars, and if you don't believe us, tomorrow we will take you to the best diamond shop in town, and they will back up our statement."

Manuel leaned back in his bar stool and ran his fingers through his hair, trying to find words. He once again looked down at the diamond sitting on the counter. "All right. But no damage to the caves, and we do it my way and on my time."

"As long as we are in the cave by midnight on May twenty-eighth."

"Deal." They shook on it.

So Trinity and Jacob had bought their ticket into the secret caves for the needed days of the crossover, the window that would, take them back to 1755 and a waiting ship that would be in the same place, but 261 years in the past. From there they would head home, to La Palma to set history straight again and wait for the day they would leave this world.

Trinity hugged Manuel. "Thank you. You will never know how grateful we are for this." She smiled at him.

Jacob shook his hand.

"Thirty thousand?" Manuel said.

"Sí, thirty thousand," Jacob said.

Manuel smiled back at them. What did he really think of these two strange people and their strange friends? Who knows, but this was more money than Manuel would set his eyes on for the next year. It was worth risking his job, and really, who were they hurting?

May 27, 2016

In less than twenty-four hours, the eight time travellers would embark on the return to 1755. On March 14, they stepped into this world for the first time, and now, seventy-five days later, they would be leaving for the last time. As Trinity stood in her bedroom packing only the needed items, she looked at the items she had collected. She looked at all the books and clothes. None of it could go back with them, only the necessities. She, like the others, would have to return to the way things were. She liked it here, but she also looked forward to returning to a quieter time and place by the sea.

The children were also packing. For them it was a struggle. Everything they had needed to go. Everything to them was a treasure, a keepsake. In a few weeks, much of the stuff they had would no longer be of any use, but for now, it was special to them. Trinity knew it was like giving children candy and then taking it away again. They would cry, but in time move on with life. They would grow, have families of their own, and tell stories of this wonderful future world, which in time would fade from their minds.

Jacob met with the homeowner and paid him the last of the money owed to him. He thanked him for his kindness and support over these last six weeks. They wished each other the very best in the coming years.

By six o'clock, they had their last meal in Puerto Maya. For the next few days, they would survive on freeze-dried camping food and bottled water. Lanterns would provide them light. They would sleep on air mattresses, waiting for the moment the crossover came. Like at the Marble Caves, they could not step outside the three field gate generators. If they did, they could miss the crossing and never return home.

After dinner, they boarded the van that would take them to the Secret Caves. Before doing so, Jacob checked the gates and graphene computer one last time to ensure they were fully charged.

Jacob looked to Trinity. "Ready?"

Trinity paused, thinking. "Yes, ready."

The doors to the van closed, and they departed for the caves and the long wait ahead.

Good-bye, Puerto Maya; good-bye, Mexico; good-bye, Chile. It was a challenge; it felt amazing to be alive again. To test one's soul, one's spirit, to prove we still had what it took to make that next hill, the next river. What lies ahead will test who we are even more.

May 28, 2016

The eight met Manuel just after 9:00 p.m. They greeted each other, and then he took them and their supplies and equipment into the caves. After a short, breathtaking twenty-minute walk, they came to the spot Jacob had recorded from the computer. The good news was the location was out of the water—well, most of it was. Jacob had been worried that they would be sitting in water for the next few days. The area in question was yellow in color, with stalactites hanging from the ceiling. The water around them was crystal clear, and they could see all the way to the bottom of each water hold. The air was warm. It felt good.

"Funny," Manuel said.

"How so, Manuel?" asked Trinity.

"When the caves were first discovered in 2009, the owner thought he was the first to find them and explore them. But when they started to map the caves, they found a number of backpacks and camping equipment abandoned around this area. We never could figure out how they got into the cave or what happened to the people who left them. I was told they were all covered in silt, like the packs had been here for a hundred years or so."

Jacob walked past him. "Excuse me. Really interesting."

Trinity jumped in. "Did they find any dead bodies down here when they found the camping gear?"

"Ah, no."

"Good," Trinity said. "This is a good thing."

They started to set up camp. Trinity and Jacob thanked Manuel and asked him not to check back on them until the sixth day. Under no conditions could he or anyone else come and see how things were going.

Manuel looked at them for the longest time. Only God knew what he was thinking. What would Manuel find in six days? Two families ready to return to the world above or two families who had killed themselves in the name of their religion? Manuel didn't know, but he would respect their wishes, hoping for the best. The whole thing was just too strange.

After Manuel left, the first thing Jacob and Tom did was set the three field gate generators in the triangle pattern as they had in the Marble Caves. Then they settled in for their first night. With luck, they would be gone sooner rather than later.

May 29, 2016

Today was like the last day. Nothing happened. The children just read books, Trinity looked at photos and listened to music. Keara and Tom sat and watched DVDs on a small player they bought in Mexico. This would be the last time they would watch a movie. It was fun to see what they had missed these last couple years.

Jacob slept, or would look at magazines, reading about what was new in science. News, on the other hand, was of no interest. It would no longer matter. If there was anything of interest, it was history. But even this was of little use now. When you are given the exact date of your death, you start not caring or dreaming anymore. Jacob now just wanted to spend the last few years with his family and children to watch them grow, be happy and safe.

May 30, 2016

Just after midnight, as they slept, came the sound and the taste in their mouths. Trinity awoke first, dazed. She called out to Jacob.

"Jacob, it's starting!"

Jacob awoke in shock. "What? Are we all here?"

Jacob stood and quickly looked around to see if there was anyone missing or if someone had wandered off. If their children were younger, this could have been a concern, but they knew the risk and for this reason would not step outside the triangle.

Keara and Tom awoke and started to look around, trying to take in the event. Next the children started to stir.

Just as the very first time in the cave in Nordegg, on March 24, 2014, the lights went out. They sat silently in total darkness. Bianca screamed. This was new to her and the other children; the last time they had crossed, they sat in caves that still allowed for outside light to drift in. But this time, they were in complete darkness.

"Quiet!" yelled Trinity.

"Wait for it," Jacob said.

Then it came, the glow, the greenish glow, the fluorescent band of light that started on one side of the cave and then swept through and over them. It enveloped them and carried them.

Then darkness, total darkness. There was not a sound, just silence. Finally, after a few seconds, you could hear the sound of a light stick being broken. Jacob shook the stick to bring it to life. The green glow reflected off their faces.

"Are we all here?" Jacob asked.

"Did it work?" Trinity asked.

"One can hope, can't see why not. We went somewhere, just hope it is 1755 as planned."

The others broke light sticks to provide some added illumination. Jacob pulled out a windup LED flashlight and started to charge it.

Bianca pointed. "Look, the water is up in the cave around us."

Jacob took the LED light and walked over to the water. "Yes, about five feet."

"Is that going to make it hard to get out? There was that one place where the water was almost to the ceiling," Tom said.

"No choice, we will have to swim underwater if we have to."

They started to pack up the camping gear and field gate generators. "Only take what we need. The rest can stay behind. Tom, can you help with the computer and generators?" Jacob asked.

"Bianca, Christopher, help me with the packs. You each have to carry one," Trinity said.

After thirty minutes, they were ready to leave. They had what would be needed in the next few days as they headed to the coast to continue waiting.

Their head lamps were useless since the shift had once again drained all the batteries of their power. The only light now was the glow sticks and the windup LED flashlights each of them had. Each of them carried a backpack. The children had smaller packs and Jacob and Tom the largest. In his backpack, Jacob had the computer and field gate generators enclosed in plastic to protect them from the water.

Soon they came to the spot with the low ceiling. Sure enough, the water was right up to the top.

"How far was this stretch?" Tom asked.

"Not sure. Fifteen, twenty feet?" Jacob replied.

"I can't do this," Trinity said.

Jacob looked at Trinity. "Sorry, dear, you have survived a lot more than this. Failure is not an option now." He stopped to look at the water blocking the cave. "Good news, the water is crystal clear. Just don't stir up the sediment, and we should see fine."

Jacob turned to Tom. "You first, Erich next, followed by Josh, then Keara." As he talked, he pulled out a rope and handed it to Tom. "Tom, tie this rope to you. Once you are on the other side, pull. Then Erich will follow. Erich, look at me. Once your dad is on the other side, take a deep breath and then pull yourself through the space as fast as you can. Got it?"

Jacob turned to the others. "Leave your packs. Once most of us are through, we will pull the packs through, one by one, using the rope. The last thing we want is the packs slowing us down or getting hooked on something." He looked at Erich. "Ready?"

"Ready," Erich said.

Tom started out first. He took a deep breath and then went into the water. Sixty seconds later, there was a tug on the rope.

"Your dad is on the other side. Your turn, Erich," Jacob said.

Erich followed, as did the others. When it was Trinity's turn, she looked at Jacob.

"Good luck, dear," he said.

Trinity took a breath and dove down under. She pulled herself through the space toward the light on the other side. The water was clear, and she could easily see where she was going. As she neared the end, she found that she was running low on air. Her lungs started to strain with pain, the walls of the cave were starting to close in on her, but she would have to make it. Then there was a hand. Bianca pulled her mother from the water. Trinity came out gasping for air.

"You OK, Mamá?" Bianca asked.

Coughing, Trinity stepped from the deep water and looked at her daughter. "I'm good, Bianca. Thank you."

They then pulled the packs and the other equipment through the waterway.

"I hope the computer doesn't get wet," Trinity said.

"Me too," Tom replied.

Finally, after fifteen more minutes, Jacob came up gasping for air. "Shit, that was not easy," he said.

Once again they pulled on their packs and headed off toward the location where the entrance should be. They had finally arrived.

"This should be it," Jacob said, looking at the map and then up to the ceiling.

They could see tree roots all around them. Jacob and Tom dropped their packs and pulled out two small shovels. They then worked their way up to the rooted ceiling and started to dig at the roots. Trinity, Keara, and the children looked on.

An hour later, they were still digging. The first set of glow sticks had died out, and they were now on to new ones. Tom and Jacob were now taking turns to dig.

"Holy crap. How deep are we?" Jacob said. They had dug a two-metre hole in the ceiling.

Trinity and Keara started to get concerned.

"Tom, take over." Jacob dropped the shovel, and Tom once again started in.

For the next three hours, they continued to dig. The water around them was now muddied with all the dirt being dumped into it. They were out of glow sticks. If not for the LED flashlights, they would be in total darkness.

Then there was the first sliver of light.

"Yes!" Tom yelled out.

"Thank God," said Trinity.

Tom worked for a few more minutes, and the sliver of light turned into a hole and then finally an opening that would allow for their escape.

From the floor of the jungle, a hand came into view. Next to the hand walked a small black tarantula. Finally the face of Trinity emerged. She was the first to step forth from the underground world into the fading light of the end of day. All around her was thick jungle and the sound of animals. She rolled onto her back and looked at the sky for a minute, and then there was the call from below to take hold of the packs.

By the last light, the eight sat on the jungle floor, looking at their new world. Tomorrow they would get their bearings and start to head to the coast, a trek that would take them about two hours.

Tonight they would sleep under the stars. Jacob and Tom tried to start a fire, but the jungle wood was just too wet, and they couldn't keep the fire going. Their sleeping bags were soaked from the underwater crossing. Their start to the new timeline was not going as planned, but they had crossed over. The question that would be answered in the coming days was to what year and what exact date?

Jacob held Trinity as the two slowly drifted off to sleep with their children by their side.

Unknown Date

At first light, they started to pack to head toward the coast. They ate some freeze-dried food and changed out of their caving clothing into clothing better suited to their new time. It was a mix of twenty-first century that could pass for 1755. Once they made the coast, they would, with luck, find their ship and once again blend into the world around them.

They headed east to the coast. The trek was horribly slow, the jungle thick, but by late afternoon, they stood looking out at the sea. The plan was for the *Semper Fi* to sail up and down the coast for the next two weeks, between Cozumel and the coastline. They would start a large fire and keep watch for the ship. With luck, the smoke from the fire would be seen for miles, and the *Semper Fi* captain, Correa, would see it and come in.

Now the question was, was it the right year, the right week? If not, they would be all alone. No ship would be coming. The first time they crossed into 2016, they had hit the mark. Was it the same this time? Did they arrive the last week of September as planned?

Even if they did, there was a chance the ship was delayed or just not coming. If this was the case, they would be stuck, marooned on the shores of Mexico, or New Spain. Unlike the twenty-first century, with all its towns and resorts, in 1755, there was nothing—no towns, no settlements—that they knew of or could map. Their only hope would be to head south down the coast to Belize City, a British town that would someday become the country of Belize. It was a distance of around five hundred kilometres, a walk that would take twenty-one days, if they were lucky. Could they still do it? Could the children do it? Fifteen years ago they did this and more, but that was then. As Trinity once said to God in prayer, "Thank you for making us young and foolish, not questioning what we can or cannot do." Now they were older and full of doubt, full of all the reasons things cannot be done.

Jacob was trying to start the fire on the beach, but the wet wood and leaves wouldn't burn. Tom walked up to Jacob and handed him a flare.

"What's this?" Jacob asked. He took the flare and looked at it. "Thanks, a little ahead of the times. If we use it, there will be a lot of questions, and I hate questions."

"Fine, but just in case. I'd rather be found sooner and deal with the questions later."

Trinity, Keara, and the children sat on the beach looking out at the sea. Trinity turned and called back to Jacob, "Why are there no people living here at this time?"

Jacob looked up from the smoke. "Ah, that is because the jungles are full of Mayan natives."

"What? How is it you forgot to tell us that part?" Trinity snapped.

"What would the point be? Not as if we could find another crossing point in time. This was the one; we had to deal with it."

"Are they safe?" Keara asked.

"Wouldn't know."

"You know that smoke will be pulling them in from miles around," Tom added.

"Oh, this isn't smoke yet. Once we see the ship, I plan to put all this green crap on to get a lot more smoke."

"You didn't answer my question!" Keara said.

"What? What do you want me to say? I hope they leave us alone. I hope the ship is only a day off. They should be making a run once or twice a day up and down the coast. And I hope by tonight or tomorrow noon, we are aboard."

"I hope so!" Trinity said.

Tom walked over to Jacob. "What if she's right and the local natives come and pay us a visit?"

"Then I hope they are friendly."

"And if not?"

Jacob pulled his shirt up. In his belt were two 9mm pistols he had purchased on the black market in Mexico the second week they were there.

"You have spare mags with those?"

"Sí, I do, one for you and one for me, with three spare mags. If we have to use them, I hope, they get the point and then back off."

"If that was to happen, would we not be changing time or history?" Tom pointed out.

"What, how can you change it? What happens was meant to happen. Written in the stars before you or I were ever born." Jacob smiled. "Let us hope that in the stars, there are no local natives coming our way."

That afternoon was hot and sunny. Trinity and the others wanted to head inland to stay out of the direct heat, but Jacob wanted them close. He was worried about what could be waiting in the jungle.

Finally dusk came to the sea. The only light for the evening would be from the beach fire. They would take turns keeping it going. With luck, in the night, the ship would pass them by and see the fire burning onshore.

That night, no one could sleep. They sat around the fire, keeping warm. Tom and Jacob would take turns sitting on the beach, away from the fire, so they could preserve their night vision. Next to the fire they were blinded and couldn't see into the dark as clearly. There was also the noise of the burning wood. Away from the fire, they could hear the sea and, most likely, a passing ship.

Just after three in the morning, most of the group were in and out of sleep next to the fire. It was Trinity's turn to keep watch for the passing ship. She sat there as the waves washed in at her feet. The good news was the moon was one day away from being full. She could see for miles out to the sea. As she sat there, she thought she could hear the sound of a bell. She turned her head and then stood up, looked out at the open water. She then pulled out the binoculars she had to have a better look. She kept looking right and left. The moon was in her face, and it didn't help, as it made it hard to see a ship that would have only the light of a small lantern to show it off in the darkness.

Then finally she thought she saw something, a light, a shape. She walked closer to the water and looked again. Yes, there it was—a ship, a two-masted ship.

"Yes, the *Semper Fi!*"

Trinity turned and started to run up the beach toward the others.

"Get up, get up! It's the ship. Get the fire going as big as you can."

Jacob awoke and started to look around. "Tom, the fire!"

Tom started to throw on wood and dead leaves to get it to build in size. There was more smoke than fire, and Tom was looking for air to breathe.

"Oh, screw it." Tom pulled the small pocket flare out, held it to the sky, and pulled the string to fire it. The flare fired and raced into the dark night sky.

Jacob looked up to the sky and then down at Tom.

"Screw it. Tell them you found it in China in one of your trips there."

Jacob ran down to the water with Trinity by his side. He asked for the binoculars and used them to look for the ship. From the view of the binoculars, he could see a man waving a lantern from right to left.

Jacob turned and called to Tom, "Tom, bring me a burning piece of wood I can use as a torch."

A minute later, Tom ran up behind Jacob with the torch. Jacob stood there waving it back and forth.

Then the ship dropped its sail, changed course, and started to head toward the coast.

Two hours later, the eight time travellers stood on the deck of the *Semper Fi*, shaking the hand of Captain Correa.

"Gracias," Trinity said to the captain. "Gracias!"

The captain lifted his hat with a smile in a gesture of "You're welcome."

And so they were once again in their own time. They had made it. They had crossed time not once but twice now. They had seen the future and returned to the past. Now would come the test to see how the children would deal with going from having everything to only what they needed.

Trinity stood looking out at the coastline and watched as their fire started to die out on the beach. Jacob walked up beside her and held her. She put her head on his shoulder and smiled at him.

"Thank you," she said.

"Nothing to thank. We did this together, all of us," Jacob said.

Trinity turned and kissed him like she had not kissed him in months. "I love you." They embraced each other and continued to kiss.

Slowly the fire and the coastline drifted off in the distance, never to be seen again.

Later that night, Trinity sat next to her two children as they slept in their beds. She loved her children, but knew she had only a few more years to hold and cherish them. Soon history would take her and Jacob away from them. What was clear was everything was playing out as it should. They were all heading toward their destiny, and nothing they did would change this.

Before leaving, she kissed each of them on the forehead and said a silent prayer for them.

September 24, 1755

The *Semper Fi* headed northeast out to sea. In a day it would reach Havana. Trinity spent the morning at the bow of the ship, looking out to the open water. On the horizon was the coast of Cuba, and then Havana. The last time she saw Havana was in January 1741. She thought back to her time there, lost friends, loved ones. They would stop for a few days to get resupplied, and she and the others would make a point to once again pay a visit to Don Francisco and his wife, Doña Claudia. He was the governor of Cuba in 1741, and he and his family had taken in the weary time travellers after the sea battle with the British that took the life of their dear friend Kim.

She looked forward to the thought of seeing old friends. She also hoped there may be news of Andy Taylor. He disappeared that night the *San Ignacio* burned in Havana Harbour, never to be seen again. She knew he was still alive. The drawing of Andy and the African woman provided this. They had tried to use the graphene computer to find Andy in history but no entry could be found for him, it was as if he was lost to time.

Keara made her way next to Trinity. The two just sat there, not saying anything. The wind was in their faces, and it felt good. The same thoughts passed through Keara's mind. What would Cuba be like all these years later? Tomorrow they would know.

September 25, 1755

This morning the *Semper Fi* sailed into the port of Havana, Cuba. Standing on deck were the eight. The day was beautiful; the sun shone high in the clear blue sky above.

Trinity looked at Jacob and the children. "The last time we were here was in 1741."

Bianca looked to her mother. "This is where Don Francisco lives?"

"Yes, I want you to meet him and his children. They are most likely all grown up now, but still."

As the *Semper Fi* continued to sail into the port, Trinity looked up at the hill on the east side of the harbour; in these hills was the home of Francisco. On this beach they stood watching the night the *San Ignacio* burned and sank. A flood of memories started to come back to her.

"How much longer before we dock?" Trinity asked.

"Soon, dear, soon," Jacob responded.

Trinity just wanted to get off and see her old friends again. She wanted to see the look on Francisco and Claudia's faces. She wanted to once again walk in the garden and the stable of the estate home. She wanted to see the room that overlooked the harbour below.

Just after lunch, the *Semper Fi* found her place at the dockside. For the next four days, the ship would remain docked as the eight started their search for old friends.

On this day, I once again stood in Havana. I looked at all the sights. The city had changed. It was not the Havana I recorded on my iPhone. It was busier; the slave trade was still strong. This was the one thing I could not stomach living in this time. All one could do was his or her own small part to give these people the dignity and freedom all people deserve in life. I looked forward to getting a carriage and riding around the bay to the hills east, which overlook Havana Harbour. There I would find the home of Don Francisco and Doña Claudia, I hoped they would still live there. If not, perhaps the new owners could tell us where they now resided.

Trinity and the others found two carriages to take them into the hills of Havana; with luck, they would make the estate well before dark. They set out and headed south then east into the hills. The carriages were drawn by four black horses each. This brought back memories of their stay here all those years ago.

Jacob sat by Trinity's side, the children across from them. Bianca and Christopher could feel the excitement through the eyes of their parents. As they road up into the hills, Trinity and Jacob started to have a bad feeling. The streets that once were so well kept were now in very poor condition. The homes on each side of the street were old, rundown, and in disrepair. Trinity looked at Jacob, who in turn showed a look of sadness.

Just after 4:00 p.m., the carriages came to a stop at the ruined gates that were once the entrance to the estate home of Don Francisco and Doña Claudia. Trinity's and the others' hearts were broken at the sight. Trinity slowly stepped from the carriage and walked toward the open gates. She was followed by the others. As they walked through the gates, they were met by a shell of a home, the roof long since gone from the years of storms and neglect.

They made their way into the once-great estate home. They stood in the main hall, which had once been filled with paintings and artwork from all around the world. From there, they stepped into the once-grand library, the room where Jacob came up with his plan to sail to South Africa and find diamonds. Now the walls were bare. The desk, at which once sat the most powerful man in Cuba, was gone, replaced by dead leaves across the stone floor. Trinity looked at Jacob and the others; she tried to hold back the tears.

She walked from the library and went down the hall toward her and Jacob's old bedroom. As she walked into the room, she saw there were still the rotting remains of the bed they slept in. The mattress was long gone, and only the wood frame remained. In this bed, Trinity and Jacob had conceived Bianca. A small yellow bird flew into the room from a hole in the ceiling. She looked up at what remained of the ceiling. She could still just make out the shape of the painting that adorned it, which was of God and Heaven. She would lie here at night and look up at that painting and think of her lost friends. She walked across the dirt-covered floor and looked out the window toward the sea.

She started to cry. Jacob came to her side and held her tight.

"Sorry, Trinity."

That night they all sat looking out over the harbour below. The lights from all the ships were as they remembered it. The drivers of the carriages patiently sat nearby, waiting to return to Havana and their families.

As they sat there, a man came walking up to them in the dark. He asked what they were doing here. Jacob told the man they were just looking at the sights below. The man looked at the four adults, then stepped forward and held up a lantern to Trinity and Keara's faces. He paused and then said, "Trinidad?"

"Sí, soy Trinidad," Trinity said.

It turned out the man was one of Don Francisco's servants from all those years ago. His name was Hector Vargas, and he was there at the time Trinity and the others lived with Don Francisco that fall of 1740. Jacob looked at the man and then remembered him from the stables.

Hector asked if the eight would come and join him and his family for dinner. They had very little, but he would be so honored if they would come. They looked at each other.

"Sí," Jacob said.

So the eight and the two coach drivers headed up the small path toward Hector's humble home. The house was a small three-room building made from whatever he could find from the surrounding buildings. They were introduced to his wife Gabriela and two children, a boy named Pedro and a girl named Adela, who were about the same age as Erich and Bianca.

The home was not what any of the travellers were used to, but the welcome for dinner was from the heart of this man and woman. For the next hour, they all sat together around a very small table with only the light of the few lanterns they had along. The only food was bread and some chicken, which they all shared between them.

Trinity asked what became of Don Francisco. Hector went on to tell the group that Don Francisco died a few years after Trinity, Jacob, Keara, and Tom left Cuba. His wife, Doña Claudia, and children returned to Spain, and the new governor of Cuba didn't want to live on this side of the harbour, but preferred the centre of the city. The home was left abandoned.

Trinity sat there looking at the man. She thought back to the days with Doña Claudia and her children.

Then Hector said. "¿Sabe usted algo de Andy?"

Trinity said, "What about Andy?" in Spanish to Hector. Keara and the others turned with interest toward him.

Hector went on to tell how, in 1748, Andy returned, also looking for Don Francisco. He came in the summer and had with him a young African girl by the name of Grace by his side. He told him how Andy had aged, but looked very good and happy. Trinity and the others wanted to know more.

157

Hector told them that Andy was living near Villa Nueva de Santa Clara, in Eastern Cuba, on an estate he and Grace had built. He was growing tobacco and doing very well.

Trinity looked to the others. They all knew that look.

Jacob said, "Yes, tomorrow we will leave for Santa Clara."

After one more hour, they finally said their good-byes to this man and his family. For the food and conversation, Jacob pulled out three gold coins and gave them to Hector. These gold coins were more money than he would see in a year.

"Ah, gracias, muchas gracias," Hector kept saying over and over again as the group left.

Trinity turned to the man. She hugged him. "No, gracias a Usted, Hector."

They departed in the night and returned to the two carriages to return to Havana. As the coaches departed, Hector and his family walked up to the road and waved good-bye to the travellers. Trinity lifted her hand and waved a final farewell.

By midnight, the carriages pulled into the docks and dropped off the riders. Jacob paid the two men very well for their help and for the long day they put in. He asked if they could arrange to have eight horses and a guide for the morning so they could ride east to Santa Clara. The men said they would see to it.

Then they boarded the *Semper Fi* for the night. Trinity was sad to hear what had become of her old friends, but she now hoped that in the next days she would once again see the face of Andy Taylor. She hoped he was happy now with Grace by his side. He deserved happiness and hoped he had found it.

They returned to their cabins and went to sleep looking forward to what tomorrow would bring them.

September 26, 1755

By first light, a team of men showed up with eight fresh horses the time travellers would use to ride east to Santa Clara.

Trinity and the others started the day with breakfast and said their good-byes to the ship's captain. With luck, they would return in six or seven days. The captain wished them luck and would wait for their return.

The group would be joined by two Spanish guides who knew the island. The journey was just over three hundred kilometres and it would take three days. They rode out of the city and headed east along a dirt road that would take them to a number of towns along the way. The going was level, so each day they would make good time. The guides took the lead followed by the eight. Trinity looked forward to seeing Andy after all these years.

That night they spent their first evening at Matanzas, a town dating back to 1572. They found a small inn for the night. They were all tired from the long day of riding.

That night everyone slept well. Morning would come far too quickly.

September 29, 1755

By noon the ten travellers rode into Santa Clara. Now they would have to ask around if anyone knew an Andy Taylor, plantation owner.

They started their search at the town hall and very quickly they knew of a Don Taylor, who lived some fifteen kilometres southeast of the town, on a plantation next to Don Estévez.

Trinity couldn't wait. The others wanted to stop for lunch, but she wanted to push on.

I couldn't wait any more. Fourteen years ago was the last time I saw my friend Andy. After the loss of his wife, and

my best friend, Kim Wong, Andy was never the same. I
hoped he had moved on and now found peace and happi-
ness with Grace.

After a brief argument, it was decided they would first eat and then carry on. By night they came across the estate of Don Estévez. They called at the gate of the massive estate, asking if they knew of a Don Taylor. A servant came down to open the gate and see what they wanted. After a short conversation, they were invited in for the night.

They were met by Don Luis Estévez and his wife, Estela, and their three children. They invited the travellers in for dinner and a place to spend the night.

"Gracias, por lo tanto sería un honor," Trinity said to Estévez.

That night they sat around the grand dining room table as the seven children played together in other parts of the house. Trinity finally asked if they knew of an Andy Taylor and a woman by the name of Grace.

Don Estévez sat there. He turned to his wife and then looked back to Trinity and the others. He asked how they knew him.

Trinity went on to tell Don Estévez how they were friends of his from fourteen years ago and how he had run away on the morning of January 2, 1741, never to be seen again, how they thought he was dead for all these years.

Don Estévez cleared his throat, then spoke the words no one wanted to hear.

We were too late; we had missed our friend by three years.
He had died on September 22, 1752, from a wagon accident.
Don Estévez told us how he met Andy on the road leav-
ing Santa Clara and how he offered him a job. He told us
how he saved the life of an African slave girl and named

her Grace. How he was loved by all those around him. How in his last days here he still had an everlasting love for his wife, Kim. He never loved anyone as much as he loved her.

Trinity and Keara sat there heartbroken for their lost friend. Tears formed in Trinity's eyes. She no longer wanted to cry over any life, but she couldn't help herself. Slowly all the things she had hung on to, hoped for, wished for a happy outcome for, were fading away at every turn. Bianca stepped into the room and saw her mother crying. She came to her side and asked what was wrong.

"Nothing, dear, just saying good-bye to one more old friend." Trinity wiped the tears away.

Don Estévez told Trinity and the others he would take them to meet Grace and show them where their friend was buried. Trinity smiled and thanked him.

Don Estévez then lifted a glass of red wine and made a toast to Andy. They all stood and lifted their glasses of wine high.

"To Andy, may you be at peace, my friend, and may Kim be by your side," Trinity said.

I waited years for this moment, always hoping, praying, wishing we would one day see him again. The return to Cuba was not as I hoped it would be. I hoped to see dear old friends, but I was left with only loss. But, from the loss would come closure. I hoped that the years Andy spent here living in Cuba, he was happy with Grace. I hoped together they gave each other the love they needed. I will always miss you, Andy Taylor. Be at peace, my friend. Someday we will be joining you in the afterlife. Please keep a fire burning for us so that we will one day all be together again as friends. I love you all, Andy, Kim, and Robert.

They said their good-nights and were shown to rooms for the night. Tomorrow they would meet Grace and visit Andy's final resting place.

Later that night, Trinity sat in bed next to Jacob. She stared at the ceiling, thinking. She'd had a dream to say good-bye to her family, her loved ones, but after all the miles, all the years, all the danger, she had not fulfilled it. Her heart was empty. She would leave this world without ever being able to say good-bye.

Trinity started to cry. Jacob pulled her close to his side and held her tight.

September 30, 1755

That morning, Trinity, Jacob, Keara, Tom, and the children rode into the estate of the late Andy Taylor. The estate home Andy built was quite beautiful, with white walls and a red roof, complete with a small bell tower.

From the main house stepped a young woman who appeared to be in her late twenties. She was a beautiful African woman with long black hair. She wore a white dress with fine lace embroidered throughout the garment, and a black belt with a gold buckle. Trinity sat on her horse and looked down at the young woman. She smiled, slowly stepped down, and made her introduction.

The young woman introduced herself only as Grace. Grace had this amazing white smile, which filled Trinity's heart with nothing but love. She could see right away why Andy took in this child, who had grown into a beautiful woman. Andy cared so much for her that in his will, he left everything to her. He had freed her from slavery. On this estate there were no slaves, every man, woman and child were free. The goodness Andy brought into this world was carried on by Grace and the others around her. Grace was still single; all these years later, she never left Andy's side. She ran the estate with the help and support of Don Estévez

In all the years Andy lived in Cuba, he was never able to move past his love he had for Kim. I thought how sad. But, I also understood it was a very special love the two had. Andy and Kim were soul mates; this would never change between them. Grace and Andy were two soils who now needed each other, Andy for the loss of Kim and Grace for the darkness in man's spirit for imprisoning people into slavery. It takes a special love to save someone's life. I was proud of Andy, and I was thankful of Grace for being by Andy's side. No one should be alone.

Grace took Trinity and the others around the back of the estate home to a fenced-off area with black wrought iron bars. A white stone gate marked the entrance to a grave site.

Trinity stood and looked at the gate. She hesitated for a moment and then stepped through, followed by the others. Inside there was only one gravestone shared by Andy and Kim. Kim's body was buried at sea, but still Andy had built an everlasting monument to his loving wife.

The first inscription on the stone was that of Kim. Trinity and Keara stepped forward and knelt down before it. The grave was lined with beautiful flowers that waved in the afternoon breeze. Engraved in the stone were words to friends and family. Keara read the words out loud.

"Kim Wong Taylor, Chinese Princess, beloved wife of Andy Taylor. She will always be missed."

Trinity wiped the tears from her eyes. Tom and Jacob stood in the background with their hands crossed.

Next to Kim's inscription was the one for Andy. On it the words were written: *Andy Taylor, beloved husband of Kim Wong. They are now one again.*

Trinity put her hands on the stone and started to cry like the day she lost Kim in the sea battle. She couldn't control her tears. For all these years she had held it back, but now she let go, and accepted that Andy was gone.

Grace stepped up behind her and put her hands on her shoulders.

"It's not fair. It's not fair," Trinity said. She looked to the sky and finally smiled toward heaven. "Good-bye, friend."

That night, the eight were the guests of Grace and her house staff. They sat, after dinner, looking out at the plantation Andy and she had built over the last ten years. Andy and Grace had done well. Trinity and the others now had closure.

Tomorrow, they once again would ride west back to Havana, but tonight they would spend it with a loving woman who would tell them all about Andy and all the things he had done since saving the life of an African slave girl.

The last thing she talked about was how Andy died and how a doctor came to his side in his final hours to help him with his passing. How the doctor spoke English to him, and how Andy found it difficult to communicate in English again after so many years.

Trinity and the others all looked at one another.

Trinity asked if the doctor had a name. Grace thought for the longest time, trying to think back all those years.

Then finally she said, "Markus era su nombre."

They all looked at each other. Jacob then lifted his glass of wine. "To Markus. We hope your Jessica is by your side, as Andy is with Kim."

"Cheers," they all said.

October 1, 1755

The time travellers said their good-byes to Grace and Don Estévez. They thanked them for their hospitality and support. Trinity reached into her saddlebag and pulled out a small leather notebook. From the pages she pulled the pencil sketch Markus had hung from the wall of his cabin on the *Semper Fi*. She unfolded it and gave it to Grace.

Grace looked down at the paper and then looked up at her.

"Something to remember him by," Trinity said.

Grace smiled, and then tears formed in her eyes. The two women hugged, and so ended the journey of Andy Taylor. He would be missed and always loved.

The group climbed onto their horses, waved, and turned to ride out.

Good-bye, Andy; good-bye, Kim; good-bye, Grace. It was an honor to know you all.

October 4, 1755

The eight once again boarded the *Semper Fi* and prepared to set sail for La Palma. Their mission was clear—to return their children to their home so that they could take their place in history.

That night, at high tide, the *Semper Fi* set sail from Havana, Cuba. Trinity thought back to the last time she sailed into these waters. Her heart was filled with sadness, and today, as she once again sailed out, her heart was again sad.

Good-bye, Cuba. This will be the last time I ever set eyes on you. Thank you for all the memories, good and bad.

In the distance, Cuba faded into the darkness for the last time.

October 25, 1755

The trade winds were at their backs and the ship was making great time as it got closer to La Palma Island. In six more days, they would be off the coast of their home island. Soon life would once again return to normal. The journey they took would soon fall into memory, and as the years would go by, the children would soon forget about it as they went on with their lives.

Today Trinity sat on the open deck reading a book. She found it hard to read. The tales and stories were, well, so boring compared to her own life. Each day that passed now moved her and Jacob closer to their last days. When God gives you the date you are to die, it makes it very hard to live anymore. This is how Trinity felt.

Everything has a season. And ours was now passing us by.

Trinity looked at the four children as they played happily on the deck. It was good to see that they had once again stepped back into their own time. To them, 2016 was but a dream now.

Chapter Twelve

November 1, 1755

November 1, 1755

Morning, and the *Semper Fi* was now just off the coast of La Palma. In a few hours, it would start its turn south to the Port of Santa Cruz, and home.

Trinity stood on the deck with Keara as they looked out to the sea. The wind was cool this morning, so Trinity wore a heavy white dress with a burgundy jacket to keep warm. The children were below deck, sleeping, since there was little else for them to do. The days at sea were now an endless monotony of boredom. The wind was in their faces. Trinity let her hair down, and it felt wonderful.

"We should make port this evening," Trinity said to Keara.

Just then Jacob came up on deck after finishing a late breakfast.

"How are the kids?" Trinity asked.

"Still sleeping."

"Looks like a nice day. One more day and we're home."

"Yes, one more day," Jacob agreed.

The crew was now starting their daily ship chores, scrubbing and washing down the deck. Soon the *Semper Fi* would dock, and the last thing any of the crew wanted was to be stuck on the ship any longer than they had to be. Captain Correa made his way to the wheelman and checked his heading.

Trinity pulled out a book and found her favourite place to settle in to read. She propped up a number of padded mats to build a makeshift chair. Then she leaned back and opened the book.

"Any good?" Jacob asked.

"Shakespeare?" Trinity said.

"Which one?"

"*Romeo and Juliet.*"

"No, really."

"Really."

"That was my favourite Shakespeare story in school. Such a tragedy," Jacob said as he looked at the book cover.

Trinity kept reading without looking up. "Aren't they all?"

It is then that the world changed. The first sign were some seagulls, which were flying overhead, suddenly changing course. They started to call out, crying, all at once. Jacob looked up, as did a few of the other crew members. The birds started to dance everywhere in the sky. Trinity gave it little attention as she continued to read.

Then a crew member standing at the front of the ship yelled out, "Capitán!" He pointed to the port side of the ship. "Marejada, marejada!" He yelled as loud as he could.

Trinity looked up from her book. "What did he say?"

Jacob turned and looked at the crew member pointing out to sea. He stood up and walked to the ship's rail. The captain made his way past the helmsman and pulled out a looking glass. Jacob strained to look out at the open sea. Then he could see it. The sea was rising, swelling toward them.

"Oh shit!"

Trinity looked up. "What?"

The captain called out, "Todo el timón a babor. Suena la alarma!" A sailor ran and started to ring the ship's bell as loud as he could.

Trinity's head snapped back looking at the captain, then back to Jacob.

Jacob turned toward Trinity and Keara, who were both now making their way toward the railing next to Jacob. "Tidal wave!" he called out.

"What?" Trinity said as she now looked at the open sea.

The helmsman turned the ship's wheel as fast as he could to the port side. The ship slowly started to turn left. The tidal wave was now fifteen hundred metres out and closing in fast. Jacob looked at Trinity, not knowing what to say. Trinity took hold of some of the ship's rigging, and it started to tighten around them. The wave kept growing and coming toward them. It was ten metres tall, approaching at one hundred metres per second.

"Oh my God! Jacob!" Trinity screamed.

The ship was now at a forty-five degree angle to the approaching killer wave.

Jacob yelled out, "Goddamn it, turn, turn!"

He looked back at the captain and the helmsman. The captain dropped his looking glass and ran to help the helmsman turn and hold the ship's wheel full to port. The other crew members looked on in shock at the approaching wave. Some started to run toward the back of the ship, crying out as they did.

Jacob looked at Trinity and Keara. "Listen to me! Hold on to anything you can, and don't you let go!"

The wave came racing in on them. Keara looked around trying to find something to hold on to, and as she did, she yelled out for Tom.

The ship was now almost ninety degrees to the wave, heading straight toward it.

Trinity dropped her book and grabbed hold of the rigging with both hands. As she did, she looked one last time at Jacob, who was now grabbing a rope from the ship's deck and tying it around his waist.

Then the dark monster wave was on them. The sound was deafening; the wall of water was as high as they could see; the morning sun and sky went dark. Then, in an instant, it struck the ship, like a hammer smashing down on it. The water was like being hit by a wall of bricks.

I saw the water coming; it swept over the front of the ship.
As I watched, it enveloped the crew members who tried to
run from it. They were there, then gone. I held my breath
and closed my eyes. Then darkness, nothing.

The wave smashed over the ship from bow to stern, pushing it back to starboard. As it did, it tore the masts from the ship's deck, toppling them into the sea. The ship started to roll over to starboard.

Below deck, the children had just started to awake to the sound of the ship's bell ring. Then their world was turned upside down. The ship pitched to the right, the cabin lifted, and everything started to slide from the shelves and decks. Then their bedding started to slide from the berths. They slid from their beds, smashing to the floor and then to the far wall. Everything around them came crashing on top of them. Water started to pour in, swamping them; they tried to fight for one more breath of air.

Bianca screamed out, "Mamá! Help us!"

The *Semper Fi* rolled over in the sea, 360 degrees, finally coming back upright. The deck was stripped clean, the masts smashed and piled onto the ship's deck. As the water drained from the main deck, it revealed Jacob clinging to a rope. A few feet away was Keara. She was tangled in some ropes, coughing up water as she tried to once again get her bearings.

Jacob shook his head trying to once again sort things out. As he did, he looked around for Trinity. But she was gone, nowhere to be seen.

Jacob tried to stand on the wet deck, but fell as the ship started to roll back to the left again. As he did, he hit his head. Blood started to run down his face.

The world around him started to dance in slow motion. He looked up from the deck as he lay there. A few of the crew members started to stand. Once again Jacob fought to make it to his feet. He looked for Trinity, but she was nowhere.

"Trinity!" Jacob called out.

The ship continued to rock in the rough seas. Jacob struggled to walk to the back of the ship, calling out Trinity's name.

Captain Correa stumbled to his feet. Crew members were now calling out in pain, as many were injured from being hit by the wall of water.

Jacob made his way to the starboard side of the ship, calling out Trinity's name. He looked everywhere on the ship's deck, calling for her again and again. Then he looked at the fallen main ship's mast. He followed it into the sea, and then he thought he saw something, a burgundy object tangled in the ship's rigging. He ran and leaned over the ship's rail, trying to get a better look.

There in the tangled ropes was a burgundy jacket; he knew right away it was Trinity. Jacob looked around and spotted a sailor with a knife in his belt. He grabbed it, then stood on the ship's rail and dove into the churning sea. As he came up for air, he started to swim toward the lifeless body of Trinity.

Finally he made it. He took the knife and started to cut her body free from the tangled rigging, one rope followed by another. After what seemed like an eternity, her body was free. Jacob rolled her over. She was pale, with no color. He pulled her tight to him and started to give her mouth-to-mouth resuscitation.

"Damn it! Stay with me!" Jacob called out. He then started to swim back to the ship, pulling her behind him.

From below deck, Tom stumbled onto the main deck. He, too, was all bruised and had a number of bleeding cuts all over his body. He looked around trying to find Keara. Spotting her, he ran to her side.

As this was unfolding, Jacob made it to the side of the ship and called out in Spanish for someone to drop a rope down. Two crew members grabbed a rope and, working together, started to feed it down to Jacob. They fed the rope down to him equally, forming a loop. Jacob took the loop and put it under Trinity's arms. They then started to pull her up out of the water, onto the ship's deck. A third crew member dropped a rope down for Jacob to climb aboard.

As Jacob made his way onto the deck, he saw Trinity laid out. Keara and Tom had made their way over to her lifeless body. Jacob struggled to his feet and fought his way over to her side. There he started to give her CPR. He pushed hard on her chest again and again.

"Come on! Breathe!" Jacob called out.

Keara, Tom, and the crew looked on.

"Goddamn it, Trinity, breathe!"

Jacob kept pushing as hard as he could. A minute went by, and there was no sign of life from Trinity. Slowly, Keara knelt down beside Jacob and put her hand on his shoulder.

"Back off, Keara! She's not going to die here!" Jacob yelled at her.

Jacob kept working, pushing again and again.

"Breathe!"

More time passed.

Then, Trinity coughed and started to choke. Jacob stopped and rolled her onto her side. She started to cough up water and spit it out on the deck. Keara, Tom, and the others looked on in disbelief.

Trinity choked more and threw up more water from her lungs and stomach. She started to cry as she gasped for air. Jacob tried to help her get all the water out of her body. He held her across his legs, propping her up so she could cough the last of the water out. Then she started to breathe again. Jacob picked her up and held her tight to his side, comforting her as he held her.

"It's all right. You're fine now," Jacob said as he started to cry.

Keara came down to Trinity's side and put her arms around her. Keara, too, started to cry.

Trinity slowly looked up at Jacob's face. As she did, a small smile broke out on her face.

"Thank you," she said softly.

What we found out days later was that on the morning of November 1, 1755, one of the great earthquakes of the century took place. It was a quake that later would be guessed at being 9.0 on the Richter scale. On this morning, the quake destroyed Lisbon, Portugal, flattening the city. Less than an hour later, a tsunami wave that measured twenty metres high came ashore, washing inland and then retreating back to the sea. It would kill well over one hundred thousand people this day. The force from the quake and tidal wave would be felt as far away as North Africa and England.

For me the event would forever change everything I knew and how I would go forward from this day on.

Keara stood and then looked at Tom. "The children!" she yelled.

Tom turned and ran toward the deck stairs to take him below deck.

Jacob continued to hold Trinity. Trinity had a look on her face, a look that conveyed fear. She had seen death, and it did not sit well with her.

The *Semper Fi* sat in the ocean, motionless, slowly drifting toward the coast of La Palma. At the end, seven crew members were swept over the side and lost, never to be seen again. Trinity was lucky; if not for the love of Jacob and his quick thinking, she would have died.

Trinity now sat on the deck with her children by her side, looking up at the sun. Soon it would be dark, and the concern was that the ship would wash up onto the rocks of La Palma. Next to her was Tom, Keara, and their children, safe and well. They were a little banged up with a few cuts, but very much alive.

The crew slowly moved around the deck looking for anything they could use to try to once again build a makeshift mast and sail, but the ship was flattened. Below deck, the crew was trying to get five feet of the water out from the lowest deck, but the pumps were not working, smashed like so many other things on the ship.

Captain Correa sat by the ship's wheel, looking out at the open sea. He looked like a beaten man. The drive and energy he would bring to each day was now gone, swept over the side with seven of his crew.

November 2, 1755

It was just after midnight. The eight travellers huddled together on deck. They lay there trying to get some sleep, but the visions of what had happened kept passing through their minds as soon as they closed their eyes.

Trinity lay next to Jacob, staring up at the star-filled night sky. There was no moon, only an endless sea of stars from one horizon to the next.

"How do you feel?" Jacob asked

"My chest hurts."

As Trinity looked up, she lifted her hand and opened her fingers. She looked at her hand and the stars around it. She then closed it, trying to catch the stars in her fingers. She closed her eyes as a tear ran down her cheek.

Morning came. The sea was flat, no wind. It was very rare to have a day with no wind, but this would be the second of such days. The sun was bright, and the ship slowly drifted southeast. During the night, one of the crew members died from his injuries. There was a short prayer, and his body was cast into the sea.

Trinity stood there looking on. There was no look of emotion on her face. The last time she did this was fourteen years ago, when she said her farewell to Kim. She closed her eyes and said a short prayer.

In the late afternoon, the wind started to come up, and the ship now drifted straight south. As Trinity sat looking out to the sea, she saw the corner of a book sticking out from under a pile of debris. She moved down and pulled it out. It was her copy of *Romeo and Juliet*, which she was reading at the moment the wave hit.

She picked it up and held it tight.

The children were wandering around, trying to find something to do, something to pass the time.

At a little after 4:00 p.m., a sailor called out, "Tierra!"

They all stood and looked south. There on the horizon was land. Captain Correa pulled out a looking glass for a better view.

"La Palma," he said.

Jacob walked up beside Trinity and said, "Now, with luck, the winds don't push us up onto the rocks."

As time passed and the sun started to sink in the sky, the ship came into full view of the coastline. Then, like a vision from a fairy tale, up on the high rocks, they saw their home, the fortress, the estate, with the tower that stretched high above the main house.

"Well I'll be," Tom said.

Then as they all stood on deck, there was the sound of bells ringing from the house on the cliff, the sound of men and women shouting. The wind continued to push the ship ever closer to the shore.

Then from the house came a number of men on horseback with torches burning. They started to ride down from the house toward the beach below; they used the same trail Trinity would so often use to make her way to the beach and her secret retreat.

It was surreal; on August 20, 1754, I first set eyes on this very ship, sitting here in these very waters. I wondered if ships had a soul, a spirit, for if they did, the Semper Fi *had now come home to die on the very spot I was introduced to her.*

The captain walked over to Jacob and stood by his side. "How you say, there is a God, and he has taken you home."

Jacob turned and looked at him. "Sí, he has."

A few minutes later, the *Semper Fi* ran aground a hundred metres from the black-sanded beach. The ship rocked to a gentle stop and then leaned over to the starboard side. The beach was now alive with men rushing into the water. The captain ordered the ship's anchor dropped to hold the ship on the beach.

Trinity slowly walked to the side of the ship and looked at the world around her. The sun was now setting in the west, as it did each night. Trinity looked out at the sea and sun as they met. She placed her hand on the ship's rail.

Softly she spoke. "Thank you for bringing us home." As she did, she started to cry. She closed her eyes.

For the first night in over a year, she once again was at home in her estate high above the sea. She walked into her bedroom and looked around. The room was lit by twenty candles of all sizes, which gave a warm yellow glow to everything.

She last saw this room in November 1754, almost a year to the day. Jacob walked in behind her and dropped two bags, which contained the graphene computer and field gates, to the floor.

Trinity slowly walked toward the bed and stood looking at it. "Not fair," she said.

Jacob looked up at her. "Sorry? I don't understand."

"Ten weeks, for us it was ten weeks we were gone for on the other side. And back here, it is one year. I was robbed of nine months of time, time I should have spent with my children. Nine months I now will never have with them."

"You and I still have two more years we can spend with our children," Jacob said.

"It's not enough! I wanted those months too."

There was a knock at the door, and then Cristina entered with three other women. They made their way into the bathroom and started to prepare a bath for Trinity. The women worked at filling the large copper tub with warm water.

Later that night, Trinity sat in her copper tub surrounded by candles. The warm water felt so soothing. It was over a month since she had last taken a warm bath. As she soaked in the tub, she looked out the open window at the night sky.

As I look to the stars and to heaven, I am angry at the universe and at God. No one should know the day they will die. It should only be for God to know, yet God has given us the day through a messenger by the name of Markus. A man who didn't have the courage to live, a man who ran and took his life. I long to live another day, and yet I cannot. In just over two years, my children will be alone. They will have to go on without me, without their father. Death, I now fear it. I died, and there was nothing. If not for Jacob bringing me back, I would be lost. Please God, I know you are out there. I know you exist, for you must. When I look at all the miracles I have seen in the last fifteen years. But, still, now I fear death, more than you will ever know. I just want to live.

That night, Trinity lay down beside Jacob in bed and held him. She felt safe and secure knowing he was by her side.

December 24, 1755

Christmas Eve, and all were together, but for one, to celebrate the birth of Christ. On the beach below, Trinity walked the black sands. In the background was the estate high on the hill. The sunset was in her face. As she stood there looking out at the sea, a cold wind swept across the water. She covered her shoulders with a shawl.

Slowly from behind her came Jacob walking up. He paused and then said, "We're missing you. Christmas is not the same when you are not part of it."

Trinity continued to look to the sea. "I know. I just needed some time to myself before I…"

Jacob walked closer. "Trinity, we have little time left, and I want to spend it with our children."

"Jacob, I won't stay to the end. I am going to leave this time before the day comes. I am not going to die; God doesn't want us to die. Not yet. Not here."

Jacob walked up and stood next to her, looking at the sea. "What are you going to do?"

"I was hoping you would be by my side and together we would leave this time and find a place we can grow old together."

"And what about the children?" Jacob asked.

"Jacob, I love our children more than you will ever know. But, if we die, as we surely will in this time, on the date set forth, what difference will it make? They will be without a mother and father. This no one can change. Is it better knowing your parents are dead or knowing that they live, but just out of sight, just out of touch. Just on the other side of time."

Jacob looked to her. "You tell me. You have lived the last sixteen years now knowing they are just around the corner, knowing they are alive, but still you cannot touch them or talk to them. Even when you try."

"I think it will be easier for them. Not at first, but in time," Trinity said.

Jacob stood and looked once again at the sea. "All right." He turned and started to walk away. "Just so you know, there are only two possible crossings we could use here on the island. The very last one we could use is in July 1756. What it means is you and I will lose the last year and a half we would have had with them."

Trinity stood there and then closed her eyes, fighting back the tears. "At least we will see their children grow up."

Jacob stopped and turned, putting out his hand. "Please, Trinity, come with me. Tonight is Christmas Eve, and family and friends await us. Use what little time there is to the fullest."

December 28, 1755

Jacob sat in the estate tower looking at the graphene computer. By his side were Trinity, Keara, and Tom. Keara was crying at the thought of leaving her children. But, like Trinity, she knew the end would be the same. She would not see them grow up; she would not be at their wedding, have children, and grow old. But, if she moved on, she would see what they and their children became.

"You don't have to go with us, Tom," Keara said. "You could spend the next twenty-three years with them, watching them, before your time to die."

"I know, Keara, but I have loved you from the first day I set eyes on you. I watched over you the night the bear almost took your life.

I fought beside you at sea. I watched over you on the beaches of the Orange River. Hand in hand, we walked thousands of miles together. It wouldn't be right for us now to go our separate ways. Keara, I will always be by your side. I know in my heart our children will do well. I just have to look at their mother to know that. She is strong, and ready to take on the world," Tom said, smiling at her.

Jacob sat at the desk looking at Keara and Tom. He then said, "If we...When we do this, there are very few options open to us on this island. When we cross over in July, we can only use 1881 or 1961 as a dropping-off point."

"1961 is out for two reasons. One, our presence would soon be recorded, and the Gatekeepers would come hunting for us again. And should we live long enough, we could run into ourselves, and well, that would not be good," Tom pointed out.

"Then 1881 it is," Jacob said.

"When are we going to tell the children?" Keara asked.

"Tomorrow. They need to know, they need to understand, and they need to get ready for the day so that when it comes, they are ready and strong," said Trinity.

"So I guess now we make every day count, cherish them. For there will be no more days very soon," Tom said.

Jacob leaned back in his chair and looked at his friends. "Will we be happy?"

"Who knows? We have been happy for sixteen years now. And if the day comes when we can no longer go on without our children, we can try and find a different gate to once again cross back to a future date where they are older," Trinity said.

I knew that would not be the case. A parent does not abandon their children and then return years later when it suits them. It would be unfair to return to find that your chil-

dren are older than you are. How would they look to us? How would we look to them? No, this would be a one-way trip; once we crossed over, we would not be returning to this time anymore. We could only look on and see what the world had become without us. In 1881, my Bianca and my Christopher would be long gone from this world. I would once again have to wait my turn to be by their side in heaven. I prayed there was a place for me in heaven beside my children, my mother, my father, and my friends.

Chapter Thirteen

Spring Flowers

Spring 1756

In the months since the start of the new year, Trinity and Keara had worked closely with the children, telling them about what was coming and why it had to be as it was. At first the children did not understand, but as the days passed, they knew that their parents were destined to die. The love they had for their parents now pushed them to leave, to step over the date in time that would claim them. It was better to know they were alive somewhere else in history than dead in this time.

Each day they would talk about the future, and the past. They were shown the tower and all the magic in it. They were taught to look out for each other, to be one family. Be strong, be happy. Be proud of who they are.

July 1, 1756

Today was Bianca's birthday. She was fifteen. All in all a beautiful young lady. This would be my last birthday with my first child. I gave birth to her in a cold room in Cape Town, South Africa in 1741. Now she would be on her own. She would go through life without me by her side. I loved my Bianca; I loved my Christopher. Bianca would watch over him and be the mother I could not be.

For her birthday, Jacob and I got her a silver frame, and in that frame we placed a family photo we took in Mexico while we waited to return to this time. Jacob was able to save it from the Semper Fi. *But it would be a gift she would have to hide from the rest of the world. With this photo we hoped she would always look back and remember us for who we were. Remember happy times and proof there is more than what we believe to be. Happy birthday, dear. God bless you.*

I would miss Christopher's birthday. He was born on August 15, 1745. He would be eleven. Jacob and I gave him his gift early, on the same day as Bianca. It was only fair. Jacob gave him his pocket watch, the one I got for him in Lisbon, Christmas 1742. It was Jacob's hope that Christopher would always remember his father whenever he looked at that watch.

We were left wondering if we were doing the right thing. There is little one can do from the grave, but just maybe one can help from years later in the future.

July 5, 1756

They were now eleven days away from leaving this time. They would flee to 1881 hoping that, in this time, they would be safe, hoping that they would beat the Grim Reaper. The question remained, after crossing to 1881, how many days would they have? What was to say that the universe had set aside only so many days for them, for their life in the universe? Would the day come that matched the last given day of 1757? Would they use this last day up regardless of where they were hiding in time? On this day, would they still die? Perhaps God would still call them home even in 1882. But, should they die before their time, it would be as it should be—a mystery.

Tom spent the morning with his two sons, Erich and Josh. They rode horses around his estate; he showed them all that was theirs now, where the land started and where the land ended. It was a great estate and, if well cared for, would bring a lifetime of income to them and their future family.

In the late afternoon, Tom sat with his boys on a rock cliff looking out to sea. The warm ocean wind drifted across their faces. As he looked at his boys, he started to cry.

Erich turned and took his father in his arms. "It's OK, Dad. We will always love you."

July 16, 1756

On this morning, Trinity, Jacob, Keara, and Tom packed what they would need. Like their last journey, they packed diamonds and gold coins. Trinity spent the morning packing the iPhone and the belongings from Kim and Andy into the small wooden box with the seven sets of initials carved into the lid. The iPhone she picked was the one she carried for 1,212 days. It was worn and marked, but the case she put it in was new from her visit to Santiago. It was only right. It was always meant to be sent home across the years, and so it would again. She was lucky, though. She had a second phone with all the same photos on it. It meant she could look back at her life, her friends, and most of all, her children.

She slowly closed the lid and turned and handed the box to Bianca. "It is up to you now to take care of it and pass it on to your children and their children thereafter."

"I will, Mamá. And every time I look at it, I will think of how great a mother you were to us. I will think of our journey together. I will think how lucky we were to be your children," Bianca said.

"I was the lucky one. I would trade all the wealth we have to spend one more day with you."

Bianca smiled. "It is time to go, Mamá. Your future awaits you."

The house staff helped load the wagon with the supplies for their journey. Everything that was theirs was now signed over to their children. They would now grow up overnight to take their place in the world. The house staff was told that they were leaving for Lisbon and they would return next year. Jacob had sent a sealed letter to a lawyer in Lisbon to hold for safekeeping until the start of 1757. At that time, it was to be returned to La Palma and to the children. In it, it would tell the world that Trinity, Jacob, and the others had died from sickness. And so would end the story of Trinity, Jacob, Keara, and Tom. The children would know the true story, and in the end, that is what would matter most.

Jacob shook Felipe's hand and told him to watch over the children, take good care of them, and see to their safety each and every day ahead. Felipe looked at him with a questioning eye, but agreed he would do just that and looked forward to his and Trinity's return.

"Sí, Felipe," Jacob said.

The eight boarded the wagon and horses, said their final farewell to their homes, and then rode off out the gates for the last time.

As they rode, Trinity looked back at the estate sitting next to the sea. When she saw it again, it would be 125 years in the future. How would it change? Would it still be the same place, the same home that each day welcomed them?

They rode east to the base of the Caldera de Taburiente volcano. There they would find a number of caves. One would be used to cross time.

They all worked together to carry the supplies up the mountain to the entrance of the cave. There they worked their way inside some two hundred metres, set up the field gate generators, and waited. They laid out sleeping mats and prepared for the five-to-six-day wait that lay ahead.

Trinity and the others were now ready to say their final good-byes. The children looked at them and said they were going to wait outside the circle until the last minute. They wanted to see them leave; they wanted to spend the next few hours, the next few days talking with their mothers and fathers for the very last time.

Trinity looked at Bianca and said, "Thank you for giving us one more day." She then started to cry. She reached out and hugged her daughter for the last time. Christopher came to his mother's side and also embraced her.

Over the next few days, the children would sleep outside the circle, near their parents; they would wait for the moment of the crossing.

In the coming days, the eight sat across from each other talking. They relived their journey, starting out in the Chungo Caves, then how they walked west to the sea. How Robert lost his life, how Keara almost lost hers, how they spent the winter with the Salish, how they sailed down the West Coast to New Spain.

And finally, how lucky they were to have such great children, by the names of Bianca, Erich, Christopher, and Josh.

July 19, 1756

Just after, 5:00 p.m., the time had come. As they were talking and laughing, there was the sound and the feeling that could mean only one thing. They stopped, and all knew what it meant. From opposite sides of the circle they all stood and looked at each other. Trinity wanted to run to her children, but Jacob stopped her.

She cried out, "No!"

The children lifted their hands and waved a final good-bye. Bianca started to fight back tears as she said, "Good-bye, Mamá. Good-bye, Dad. We love you more than you will ever know."

Jacob lifted his hand to wave good-bye, as did Keara and Tom.

The aurora of light started to dance around them; it welcomed them and embraced them. As the children watched, their parents just faded away into the light, never to be seen again.

The children stood there, now looking at an empty space in time. They all fought back tears. Then they turned and slowly walked out of the cave to a future they now would have to build without their parents by their side.

Bianca stopped one last time and looked back. "Good-bye, Mamá, you will always be loved and remembered."

Chapter Fourteen

1881

As the sound and light drifted away from around them, they were left standing with only the light from a few oil lanterns burning around them. Trinity fell to the rock floor and cried, as did Keara.

Jacob leaned down to Trinity, but she lashed out at him. "Leave me alone!"

They sat there for close to an hour, no one moving, just sitting there. Perhaps they hoped that the event would happen again and take them back in time to where they had left. But, this would not be the case.

Finally they picked up the field gates and the rest of their belongings and started to walk out of the two hundred–metre cave to the light of day. As they stepped into this new world, they looked around. The sun was high in the sky, and the day was bright. The days in the cave made it hard on their eyes now.

As they looked around, they saw a group of men walking toward them from the valley below. A nineteen-year-old man dressed in a white shirt and pants waved to them.

"Hola. Que bueno verlos." He said it was good to see them.

They stopped in their tracks and looked down at the man speaking to them. They did not know what to say. Trinity looked at Jacob, Keara, and Tom.

The man continued in English. "We have been waiting for you for five days now to come from the cave. We were beginning to think you would not come for you were lost in the caves."

Jacob stood there, then said, "No, we are many things, but we are not lost."

"Good, then come down with us; we have horses and a wagon for you. We are to take you to the Wilde estate home. It has been waiting for you."

Trinity stepped forward. "What? I don't understand. How did you know we would be here?"

The man turned and looked to Trinity. "We have known you would be here for over a hundred years. My great-great-great-grandmother Bianca told us that we would have to do this one thing on this very week. It was a promise which has been passed down from father to son and mother to daughter."

Jacob asked, "What day is it?"

Without even a second thought, the man said, "May 2, 1881." He waved for them to hurry up. "Come. I want to go home." He turned to the other men and spoke to them in Spanish to hurry up and get the packs from the travellers. The men ran up the hill and helped with Trinity's and the others' bags and packs.

Trinity asked the man his name.

"My name is Carlos."

"It is a pleasure to meet you, Carlos," Trinity said.

"Which one are you? Trinity?" Carlos said.

"Yes."

"I thought so. You all look very much like the painting which hangs over the fireplace in our home."

Trinity just stood there, saying nothing.

The men put all the bags and packs into the wagon and then provided horses for the time travellers to ride. Trinity and the others climbed onto their horses and then started to follow Carlos down the mountain trail toward the sea.

By nightfall, they came to the gates of the Wilde estate, the home of Keara and Tom. They looked at the gate. 125 years, and it was almost the same as the day they left it. The wood was older, more worn, but other than that, the same.

Keara and Tom looked at it. "Wow," Keara said.

The wagon and horses passed through the gate and headed down toward the sea. There was the estate home, sitting next to the sea, just like the home of Trinity and Jacob.

Keara asked, "Who lives there now?"

Carlos turned on his horse and looked back at them. "No one. No one has lived there for the last ten years now. It still has a staff, but the Wilde family now lives in England. From time to time they may stop in for a visit, but I have only seen them once in my life living here."

"Do you know what became of Erich and Josh Wilde?" Keara asked.

"No, I do not know who they are. You would have to ask the family whose house this is. Did they live here?"

"Yes, a very long time ago."

"Well, then maybe you can find them on the family tree which hangs in the main hall. Our house has one, and I have seen one in this house also."

The group finally arrived at the doors of the house. Carlos called out in Spanish for the house staff to come out and greet them. A few seconds later, a group of men and women came from the front door of the villa and greeted the travellers. Trinity, Jacob, Keara, and Tom exchanged greetings and then were taken inside.

Inside the main hall, Keara and Tom stopped and looked at their house. To them it was a week since they last saw it, but in reality, it was 125 years. Keara looked at the walls and then to the ceiling.

Trinity asked, "Is it how you remember it?"

"Yes, more or less," Keara answered.

Keara then looked at the family tree Carlos talked about. She saw at the very start her and Tom's name and next to it those of Erich and Josh. From there the names moved to wives, children, and so on. Keara smiled as she read the names. Tom stepped up beside her and read along.

Carlos walked up to them. "We have rooms for you upstairs. If you would come with me." He pointed with his finger for them to follow.

They made their way upstairs. On the third floor, they were taken to the main bedrooms.

Carlos looked at Keara. "Sorry, what was your name again?"

"Keara, and this is Tom."

"Sí, this was to be your room." Carlos pointed.

To Keara and Tom, it was no stranger to them. It was their bedroom. As they walked in, they could tell much had changed over the years, but all in all, it still had the same charm they remembered.

"You can clean up and then come and join us for dinner," Carlos said.

Tom turned. "Thank you. We will see you shortly."

Carlos turned and then walked past Trinity and Jacob. "Now let me show you your room. Follow me."

Jacob leaned over to Trinity. "Cocky ass, isn't he?"

"Oh, you think?"

They followed him down the hall to the main guest room. This was the room that was set aside for Trinity and Jacob whenever they came to visit Keara and Tom.

As Carlos opened the door to the room, they found it filled with candles burning everywhere. Trinity and Jacob slowly walked in. It was like walking into a sea of stars. It was very much like the day they last saw it in the spring of 1756. As Trinity walked forward, she saw a package sitting on the centre of the bed. Trinity picked up the package and looked back at Carlos.

"Sí, it is for you. I have not read it, but they tell me it is a fascinating story which my great-great-great-grandmother left."

Trinity pulled the ribbon from the package, and the paper around it fell away. There in her hand was a diary written by Bianca and the watch Jacob had left Christopher for his birthday. Trinity ran her hand across the cover and then pulled the book and watch close to her heart. She turned to Carlos.

"I know not who you are, or where you come from, or why you are here now, but I know the family has waited a very long time for your visit. That book you hold is a lifetime of work for my great-great-great-grandmother, Bianca Kennedy Warner. She left detailed notes on what we should do when you come; she told us that we had to make sure you were given this book. So I have done as she asked. I hope to see you for dinner." Carlos turned away and closed the door behind him.

Trinity and Jacob were left standing alone in the bedroom. Trinity pulled the book from her chest and once again stared down at the words left by her daughter 125 years later. Trinity turned and handed the watch to Jacob, who just looked at it. Trinity started to cry. Jacob stepped up and held her in his arms.

That night for dinner, there were three, Jacob, Keara, and Tom. Trinity would not be joining them. She remained in her room, sitting by the open window with candles by her side, reading the words of Bianca.

As I sat, reading the words of my beloved daughter, I started out the evening sad and heartbroken. She started to write her diary on March 24, 1759. She was eighteen. She picked this day, for this was the day the seven of us crossed over the Rubicon. At the time we thought we would never return home, but life is full of surprises.

As I read her words, I cried, but as I read more, my tears ended. And soon I was filled with joy and happiness. My loving Bianca and Christopher lived their own world of adventure. Jacob and I had shown them what it meant to live, to be free to explore, to live life to the fullest, and that is what they did.

Jacob returned from dinner and kissed me as he turned in for the night. I, on the other hand, continued to read well into the morning.

I turned each page with a desire to know how their journey of life would end.

By the time the sun came up from behind the mountain, I was coming to the end. Christopher took a wife by the name of Ana Cristina. Together they had three children, Alexandra, Teresa, and Jacob. He died at sixty-one, very happy, for he had seen the world and lived life to the very fullest. No one can ask for more.

My beautiful Bianca made her last entry at the age of seventy. She married only once, a man by the name of Orlando. Together they had two children, a boy and girl, named Nicolas and Trinity. I smiled at the thought of this. Orlando died in 1780, at sea, exploring the world. She loved him and, like so many we knew, never remarried. Hers was an undying love for this special man.

As I read, I looked over to my sleeping Jacob and thought how lucky I was and how lucky Bianca was in her life.

Thank you, God. Thank you for watching over my children. Thank you for being there when I was not. Thank you

for giving them many years here, and thank you for giving
me peace on this day.

May 3, 1881

In the afternoon, Trinity, Keara, Jacob, and Tom stood in the family tomb they had built in 1745. They stood there staring at the names of their children scratched into the stones that now marked their final resting place. Next to the tombs of their children they found their own empty tombs. But, as per their request, dates were added to their places on the stone wall.

They spent close to an hour looking at the resting places before finally leaving and returning to the world of the living. In the afternoon sun, they sat on the grass in front of the entrance to the underground tomb. No one felt like saying anything. They just sat there taking it all in. Then finally Trinity spoke.

"So now what?"

Jacob turned to Trinity. "We go on. We live. We do what our children wanted us to do—be happy and live whatever days we have ahead to the very fullest. We live as our children lived. That is what I am going to do."

As was the custom between the four, when they met for dinner that evening they all stood around the table, lifted a glass of wine to their children, and each said a silent prayer for them.

"To our children. We…" Jacob couldn't finish his words.

Keara then said, "To our children. We will always think of you. A child should never die before their parents."

The room went quiet. Finally Trinity took a sip, set her glass down, and left the dining room.

Trinity stepped out on the balcony and looked at the sea, trying to run away from her past. Jacob walked up behind her.

Trinity spoke. "Perhaps it was better to die than live each day feeling like we were traitors to our children."

"The thing is, Trinity, I don't think they ever thought of us as traitors. They loved us too much for that." Jacob turned and walked away, leaving Trinity to face the sea without him by her side.

May 26, 1881

On this day, the four were invited for a family get-together at the Kennedy Warner Estate. They dressed in their finest clothes, which had been set aside for them, and rode to their old home.

The estate home was almost like they last saw it. But now it was filled with the next generation of Kennedy Warners. As they walked to the main door, there was fear in their hearts of how they would fit in. How much did this family of today know about how they really were their connection to the past?

The door opened, and a beautiful Spanish woman by the name of Maria, welcomed them. Trinity looked at this woman and was reminded of her own mother, with the same first name.

The house was filled with love as the time travellers walked the halls. Maria introduced them as family members from northern Spain. As she did, she gave the four a wink of the eye, as if to say, "I know the real story."

The day passed as the four got to know their future generations. Keara and Tom met a few from their family line. They learned more about what became of their children, Erich and Josh. Unlike Trinity, Keara was not as fortunate to be left a diary of her children's days. Keara looked at Trinity and in some ways felt resentful toward her. She wished she would have been as lucky.

By the close of the party, Trinity and Maria walked into the study and stood in front of the great painting that hung over the fireplace, the painting of Trinity, Jacob, Bianca, and Christopher. The two just stood there.

"It is not every day one meets their great-great-great-great-grandmother," Maria said.

Trinity replied, "Are you sure that is enough 'greats' before 'grandmother'?"

Maria laughed. "All this was once yours. And being yours, we have given you access to all the wealth the family now has. You will be well cared for and looked after. The house you now live in will be your house for as long as you want it. Should you want to move on, we would understand, but until then, you are always welcome."

"Thank you."

Maria turned and gave Trinity a hug. "It is good to have you home."

Trinity started to cry. She was many things, but she was not home. She and the others were now running from destiny.

Their days here would be like living in exile. The hopes and dreams they had of growing old with their children had been taken from them. As much as they were loved, they would always be strangers from a far-off time and place, living their days out until one day they would finally leave this world for the last time.

Chapter Fifteen

Truth

April 15, 2016

The Gulfstream jet touched down at the airport at La Palma. Aboard were Maria and Carl. The door to the jet swung open, and the two walked off to a waiting white Suburban SUV. As the door closed on the SUV, Carl told the driver to take them to the estate.

They departed the airfield and headed west. Maria sat next to Carl, not saying a word. One could tell there was an anger she was holding inside her. Their search for their child had gone nowhere.

An hour later, the SUV passed the gates of the Kennedy Warner Estate and wound its way toward the sea and the cliff house. On the way there, they passed the family tomb, which was by the side of the road.

Maria yelled, "Para el coche!" to the driver, who then stopped the SUV by the main gate of the fenced grave site. Maria opened the door and stormed off.

Carl followed her, yelling, "Maria, where are you going?"

Maria just kept walking to the door that led to the underground tomb. There she stood, looking at Carl and the driver, waiting for one to get out the keys that would unlock the door to the underground world.

Carl gestured for the driver to find a key to unlock the tomb door.

Finally the door opened, and Maria walked down the long set of stone stairs to the family crypt. She stopped and looked down toward the far end where her child was laid to rest. The tomb was dark and lit by only a few electric lights that had been added in the last seventy-five years. Then Carl came up behind her and stood by her side. He was about to say something, when she stepped forward, grabbed a torch stand from the wall, and started to walk down toward the far end.

Maria stopped in front of Trinity's tomb. She looked at it and at the date written in the brass plate set into the stone face. Maria lifted the torch stand and started to swing it at the plate and stone face.

Carl ran up behind her. "What are you doing?"

"Get out of my way!" Maria yelled at him.

Maria used all her strength and kept swinging the torch stand at the stone face, hitting it again and again. The brass plate broke free and fell to the floor; then, the stone came crashing down. She dropped the torch stand and then started to pull at what stone was left blocking her way into the final resting place. As the last of the stone gave way, she stopped and just stood there.

Slowly Carl walked up behind her. They both just stood there, looking at the hole Maria had made. Finally Carl reached out, put his hand into the opening, and pulled out a book, a diary. But, not just any diary, it was Bianca's diary, the very book Trinity had read over a hundred years earlier. Carl brushed off the dust and handed it to Maria to look at and hold.

Carl then picked up the torch stand and started to swing at the tomb of Jacob; soon this stone face was also on the floor. Like that of Trinity, this tomb, too, was empty.

"They are alive. You know that now," Maria said as she turned to walk away.

Carl finally dropped the stand to the floor and called out. "We will find them. I promise you that. I will find them!"

Maria just kept walking up to the light of the day.

Chapter Sixteen

Mistakes

July 1, 1881

Trinity stood in front of Bianca's tomb, holding a small candle. She looked at her daughter's name and said, "Happy birthday, dear." She then blew out the candle.

July 20, 1881

Jacob and Tom departed the estate and rode toward the town of Santa Cruz. They wanted to see it now, 125 years later. Trinity and Keara stayed back. They were not in the mood for travelling any place past the gates of the estate.

Santa Cruz had grown and changed. The ships now called to the port were steamers. The port was busy, with shiploads of bananas and other items leaving the island for Spain and other destinations in Europe. Jacob and Tom spent a few days seeing the world of 1881, and found it a time of wonder. Unlike the 1750s, the late 1800s were a time of discovery. Anything was possible.

After three days in Santa Cruz, the guys returned to the estate, ready to move on with life.

July 25, 1881

Jacob and Tom leapt from their horses and entered the estate home. Jacob asked where the ladies were, and the housekeeper said they were upstairs sleeping.

Tom looked at Jacob. "What gives?" he asked.

The two men went upstairs.

Jacob threw open the doors to the bedroom and stormed in. "Get up, Trinity. If you plan on dying, we could have stayed in 1756."

Trinity rolled over and slowly looked at Jacob standing there. "You're back?"

"Yes, and now it's time to move on."

"What are you talking about?" Trinity asked.

"This is no longer our home. It is a place to live, but we can no longer tell the people who live here what to do and how to do it. In the last hundred and twenty-five years, they have done very well without us."

Trinity started to sit up in bed. Jacob walked over and pulled the drapes open.

"You will have all the sleep you need when you are dead."

Trinity looked at him and pulled the hair from her face. "What do you want me to do?"

"Trinity, I want you. I want us to live again. God gave us a second chance. Do not give up on it now." Jacob looked at her. "I have booked us passage on a ship which will take us to Europe, and after we see it, we are going as far away as North Africa and Egypt."

"What? You didn't."

"I did. After we left Lisbon in 1743 and settled here, we gave up seeing any more of the world."

"We didn't give up. We had to build a home and raise a family."

"Yes, and we did. That part of the journey is now over. It is time to start the next part of the journey, and for me, that journey is off La Palma. It will take us to Europe and as far east as Egypt."

"What does Keara think?"

"You know, Tom and I don't care. I don't care what you think either. I just know I…We are not going to stay here any longer."

Trinity looked at him. She smiled. "I think that would a good thing."

"Glad you are in favor. We leave in the morning."

"What? I need time to…"

"You need time to what? You came to this world with the clothes on your back. I think we can buy what we need along the way from now on. Enjoy life, Trinity. We are not out of the woods yet. We left with a year and a half before we were to die. Who knows? In a year and a half from now, we may still die. Maybe it is just one of those things in the universe that when your time is up, regardless where you hide, you die. I'm not going to sit here and find out. I'm going to see as much as I can. If the day comes which happens to be the set numbers of day in my life, and I die, so be it. At least I lived. That is what our children wanted, and that is what they gave us. Use it, Trinity. Use what they gave us. And every day, think of them; think of how they lived life to the fullest. Think of how you are going to live life."

Trinity looked to Jacob.. "As long as you are by my side."

"I will always be by your side, Trinity, until the day you and I walk this world for the last time."

Jacob hugged her, holding her close.

August to May 1882

Over the next year, the four time travellers saw Europe. They saw the sights, returned to Lisbon, and went as far north as Amsterdam. They traced their footsteps back from Seville to Amsterdam, a journey that 140 years before would take them to South Africa, to diamonds, to the birth of their children, to a special Bushman who watched over them.

It was a journey of discovery for them. It felt good to travel, to be free. God had indeed given these four a special gift. In the entire universe, they could never know how lucky and blessed they were.

After spending almost a year travelling, they ended their journey in Cairo, Egypt. There on the Nile River, they moved into a spacious home that overlooked the water. It had a grand centre courtyard with rooms that led off from all sides. The house was three stories tall, and from the roof, they could look across the city. There they lived like kings and queens. The four spent their days meeting and teaming up with archaeologists from all around Europe. They went out each day and helped survey the Great Pyramid of Giza. Egypt was ripe for discoveries.

In 1882, Egypt was in turmoil. The British and French were in control of the government, trying to manage the country's finances. Britain claimed the Suez Canal in return for money owed to them over the last twenty years. Ismail the Magnificent launched a plan to modernize Egypt with rail and telegraph in 1863, but by 1882, the gap between rich and poor was too large to manage anymore.

Each day we would go out and help with survey work on the Giza Plateau. We would leave the house first thing in the morning. Keara and I would have to cover our faces with white cheesecloth-like gauze material to respect the local customs. Once out on the survey, we could remove it. It was hard work, but exciting. We were there, working side by side with the first to do this work. It gave us a purpose to get up each morning. I had seen the Great Pyramids when I was sixteen, when my father took me to Egypt for the first time. I remember looking at and touring the Pyramids, but this was different. We were some of the first Westerners to explore them. We used our money to help pay for much of the work. The locals were friendly and kind, but still each day we could sense a change coming. It was how people looked at you. The warmth was fading; we were now talking about moving on. Jacob and Tom were now concerned about our safety.

July 11, 1882

The winds of change were coming to Egypt. On this day, the British fleet attacked the Port of Alexandria. News spread quickly south to Cairo. The four departed to the Giza Plateau, but this would be one of their last days there. As the fighting went on in Alexandria, the hatred toward foreigners grew. News spread on how Alexandria burned. The fires destroyed much of the city.

July 15, 1882

Jacob and Tom departed their home to see if they could make plans to depart Cairo, but in those days, the only way out was by rail, north to Alexandria. For now, they would be trapped in Cairo until things settled down.

July to August 1882

Each day passed like the other. If not for the news the housekeepers would bring each day, the four would be cut off from the outside world. Trinity and Keara were now prisoners in the house next to the Nile. Jacob and Tom would, from time to time, step out and venture forth, but it was just too dangerous for the women. Spending the hot summer days in the house was unbearable. The only reprieve was the afternoon breeze that would cross the Nile River and bring a cooling to the house.

Trinity just wanted to get out, to run away. Be free again. She and Keara now questioned why they came to Cairo. Back on La Palma, there was none of this. People were happy. Life was good.

Each day now there were more and more protests in the streets. It was getting to the point that even the house staff were starting to fear for their lives. Some quit, but others remained faithful, protecting them from the outside world.

September 13, 1882

On this day, the British attacked the outskirts of Cairo and began the push into the city. Forty thousand British troops massed on the city line and then advanced. Cairo was undefended, and the British advanced with little to no opposition. That night, for the first time in almost three months, Trinity and Keara could once again walk on the city streets.

September 14, 1882

Today would forever change the course of history. In the morning, Trinity, Keara, Jacob, and Tom departed the house. They all wore white as they walked up the hill to the Giza Plateau of Cairo. As they cleared the city, Trinity and Keara dropped their white cloth veils. As they continued to walk, they ran into a group of British soldiers standing next to the Great Sphinx. They paused to talk with the commanding officer. Trinity asked him a number of questions about how the battle from Alexandria to here was fought. The officer was startled by the knowledge this woman possessed.

Little did they know, that with the soldiers was a young photographer who took a photo of the group. A simple photo, but a photo of such detail, that centuries later, it would come back to haunt them.

As they departed, Jacob spotted the young military photographer moving his camera around to take a large group shot of all the soldiers standing by the Great Sphinx. The young man lifted his hat to say hello. Jacob waved in response as the four slowly walked past him.

The photographer said, "It is not every day that one sees such beautiful women as these in a place like Cairo."

"Why thank you," Keara said to the young man.

Trinity and the others moved on, never giving much thought to what had just passed.

That night, the young man returned to his place of residence and started to develop the photo plates of the day. After a short time, the glass plate that now contained the image of Trinity and the others came to life. He lifted the plate and looked at it. There in the image was Trinity, Jacob, Keara, and Tom, standing next to the officer. The young man smiled. He was captivated by the beauty of these two women. He then spent the next hour printing the photos on paper.

Once they dried, he placed them in a box and sent them off to London. In London they were viewed, catalogued, and placed into an archive for future generations.

2035

In the year 2035, the forgotten archived box was once again opened, and the now-yellow photos it contained were scanned into a computer to forever preserve them for history.

With all knowledge comes good and bad. The photos were run through a system to see if they could identify any of the people and match them to people living at the time. The goal was to find the name of the officer standing next to Trinity, but what came out of it was much more sinister. The computer started to build an image of not only the officer but of the four time travellers. After a short time, the computer came up with nothing in regard to the officer. The young woman operator was about to move on to the next set of photos when the system started to display images.

The computer operator moved the cursor around the screen and started to click where needed. Soon the computer displayed a number of historical images of women and men who matched Trinity, Keara, Jacob, and Tom. Then on the screen were the four passport photos taken of them over the years, starting in 2012 and 2016.

The woman picked up the photo and used a magnifying glass to look closer at the faces. "Well I'll be," she said.

2337

KA sat at his desk as he did every day. The religion of time was ever so sacred to him and his followers. The red-robed man once again walked in to face KA. He spoke.

"There is once again a change in the historic timeline. In our last review of new and old dates, we have found traces of the Origins in 1882, Egypt."

KA did not look up. He continued to stare at his displays. "Where are they now?"

"We are comparing information now, but there is a report of two men and two women leaving Egypt on a ship in late October 1882 for the Port of Lisbon."

KA looked up. "Are you sure it is them?"

"There was no record of these four leaving in the last backup. Therefore, we are very confident they are the Origins. Lisbon is also a good clue as to who they are," the red-robed man said.

"They will not be in Lisbon. I have studied them for fifty years now. I know them, know how they think, know their likes, dislikes. They will not stay in Lisbon. From Lisbon they will return to their home on La Palma."

"What are we to do?"

"This time they must be stopped. This time they do not have their children by their side. This time we must end their existence before they do more damage to the timeline. They have already changed it, and if they are left unchecked, they will continue to change the course of history. This time you will lead a team to 1882 and put an end to this.

Continue to look for clues, but you will find them in La Palma. I know this for certain!" KA said.

The red-robed man bowed, turned, and left the office of KA. KA stood and walked to the window and looked down on his domain.

"This time I have you."

September 30, 1882

The steamship docked at Lisbon and aboard it were the time travellers. Lisbon, the city destroyed by an earthquake and tsunami in 1755, showed no signs of the destruction. 126 years had passed, and time heals all. The one thing that was clear was how fast things change, how short people's lives are, and how fast the world around us evolves.

Trinity, Jacob, Keara, and Tom stepped from the ship and were met by the bustle of the Port of Lisbon. The city streets were alive with people as they made their way between white stone buildings with rich red roofs. From the open windows women would look down at them as they cleaned their homes. Trinity looked up at them and smiled; she turned and looked back at Jacob and the sea which stretched out behind him. The afternoon sun was high in the clear sky. Life was now moving so fast compared to what they knew and what they had left behind.

That night they spent the evening at the Lawrence Hotel, a small hotel outside of Lisbon, in the countryside. For the next few days, the four would rest, recharge their spirits, and then board a ship to return to La Palma.

That evening, Trinity and Jacob sat on the outside veranda and drank tea. The air was cool, the sky clear as they looked into the heavens.

"I must be getting old; I just want to go home and sleep," Trinity said.

Jacob sat there looking into the night sky. "Where is home?"

Trinity leaned forward in her chair, thinking about what Jacob had just said. "Where we choose to make it."

"And where is that?"

Trinity just sat there.

Indeed, where is that? Since leaving La Palma in 1756, we no longer had a home. We were just wanderers, drifting from one place to the next. We were people without a country, exiled. When I was growing up, I read a book about a man who was accused of treason in 1807. At his trial, he renounced his country, angrily shouting, "I wish I may never hear of the United States again!" For his punishment, the judge ordered the man sent to sea aboard a US Navy ship, never to return home, never to set foot on land again. He moved from one ship to the next ship and lived his life out at sea, never seeing his loved ones again, never stepping foot on land again, never being in contact with the world he knew. He finally died at sea as an old man, regretting the decision he had made. Would we die regretting our decision?

October 10, 1882

The sailing ship docked at Santa Cruz, on La Palma. Trinity and the others departed the ship and hired a number of coaches to take them west, to their home in exile.

The day was perfect, like every day on La Palma. The year spent travelling was good for the soul, but, in the end, it was only a diversion from reality.

They climbed aboard the coaches and departed. Tomorrow Trinity would once again sit on a veranda, looking at her beloved sunset, which for now would bring peace to her spirit.

October 11, 1882

Home. As Trinity walked into Keara and Tom's estate home, she once again saw the piano that was first brought to these shores in 1744. Trinity and Keara had the same piano, one for each home, so that either could play regardless of which home they were staying at. Each year on July 9, they would meet to play together, to remember how Don Carlos in New Spain gave them a chance at life and changed their world forever. The last four years of their lives, they had missed this tradition. What seemed so important each year now was forgotten. Like so many other things, is just started to drift away with the passing years.

Trinity sat at the piano and played a few notes. Keara looked on and walked away.

Jacob walked up behind her as he once did in 1740. "Will you play?"

Trinity sat there and then slowly started to play. The music was not of 1740 or 1880. It was a song she knew from her childhood. It was filled with sadness, but you could feel the hope shining through at the end. The song was "Born to Die." Keara stopped and returned back to the room. She started to cry. Tom walked up to her and held her.

That night they all sat out on the balcony and talked about the old days—how far they had come, how theirs was most likely the greatest journey of all time.

In time they returned to their rooms for the night. Jacob lay beside his wife, Trinity, and held her tight.

"Thank you for being part of my journey," he said.

October 19, 1882

This day was like so many before. Trinity rode down the coast to find her old hiding place high in the rocks above the sea. The stone steps and pad were still there, but the chairs had since turned to dust. She looked out at the sea and then pulled out her iPhone, in its special time capsule case, and started to listen to music away from prying eyes. Again she was free for a while. Her music saved her soul. It gave her the peace she needed. She closed her eyes and thought back to the way it was, her children, her parents, her friends. The universe had given her the greatest gift. Yet, she would trade it all for the way it was in 1746. But, life goes on. She would go on.

Keara and Tom spent their day walking through the estate, looking at how they could once again bring it back to life, the way it was when they had lived there. The estate had been more or less forgotten for the last twenty years. The trees were overgrown. It was only the house that had been cared for, awaiting the time travellers' return.

Jacob sat reading books in the study, trying to plan his next move. It was the age of discovery; steam engines were coming into their being. Jacob dreamt of all the things he could do with the knowledge he had. The thought of building big, interesting things fascinated to him. Jacob loved mechanical things. He never did understand how a computer worked, but something that was mechanical, well, that was a different story. The next thirty years would be of great excitement to him.

As he read, he moved towards the window to let more light in on the pages of the book. Age was catching up to him. He once again needed new glasses to see the words on the pages. As he sat there, he noticed a large Chinese style sailing ship with flat sails and two main masts, just off the coast at anchor. He thought back to the first day they saw the *Semper Fi* in these same waters. She was now long gone, just one more page in history.

Trinity, sitting listening to music, also spotted the ship. It gently rolled in the waves. She, too, thought back to Markus and how his crew rowed him ashore that fateful day, the day that would change everything, the day that would prove how mortal they really were. She thought about her death and how October 23, 1882, would be the same number of days she was left with when they crossed over on July 19, 1756. She thought to herself that perhaps on October 23, the universe would say enough is enough; you were given your time in the universe, time to move on and give others a chance. Would she awake on October 23, only to die later that day? Soon she would find out. If she survived to live another day, then she was free from that day forward. She would be free of knowing her last days. She could live life in the knowledge that the only one who knew the answer was God.

At 5:50, the sun set at sea. Trinity returned home to the estate house just in time to see the sun dip into the sea.

The four met for dinner, full of hope and plans of the future. They lifted their glasses to what lay ahead.

The room was surrounded with a hundred burning candles. That night they took turns playing the piano and dancing with husband and wife. Trinity would play as Tom and Keara danced, and then it would be Trinity and Jacob's turn. Trinity and Jacob danced hand in hand. The house staff looked on and then finally joined in. That evening was a fitting end to a day full of hope and future promise. Once October 23 passed, Trinity felt she would be free to move on. She so badly wanted to break the cycle of time she was running from.

At just after midnight, the four departed the dining room as the last candle was blown out and walked the long curved staircase that led to the bedrooms on the third floor. The soft ocean wind blew inland from the west.

The moon was half full, the sky clear. The window drapes slowly drifted in the breeze. Trinity lay down next to Jacob, holding him.

Keara and Tom also found themselves side by side in bed, at peace, still in love after all these years. As Tom said, he would always be at Keara's side.

Outside the house, on the beach below, eight masked figures dressed in black moved from a beached boat. The figures were not of this time or this world; they carried state-of-the-art weapons from the future. They quickly moved cross the beach and shifted into the shadows.

Just after 2:00 a.m., the figures crossed the grounds of the house and approached the side entrance. They split into two teams. As the house slept, the side-entry door lock was lifted, and the door swung open. Eight black-hooded figures crossed into the hall and slowly moved in single file.

Keara and Tom slept hand in hand, not knowing the danger that was now moments away from them.

Back in Trinity and Jacob's room, the sound of the ocean waves could be heard from the open balcony doors. Jacob awoke and rolled over, glancing over at Trinity. He then looked at the open French doors that led to the balcony. The room was cold; the October night air brought a chill to the room. Jacob got out of bed and made his way over to close the doors. As he did, he paused and looked out at the Chinese ship at anchor as it rolled in the night waves. For an instant, he thought he saw a very bright flashlight, not a lantern, but a flashlight. Jacob stopped, stepped from the door, and went to the desk in the corner of the room and opened the bottom drawer. From it he pulled the set of binoculars he had brought back from 2016. He returned to the balcony. He focused the binoculars and watched the ship. There it was again, a man dressed in black walking the ship's deck, in his hand a small LED flashlight.

"What the hell?" Then it came to him. Jacob turned and ran over to Trinity. "Get up! Trinity, get up!"

"What?" Trinity asked.

Jacob started to dress. "Something isn't right."

"What? What's wrong?"

"That ship has a man walking around it with an LED flashlight."

Trinity looked to Jacob. "Oh shit!"

"Yes, get up. Get dressed. I'm going to wake Tom and Keara." Jacob returned to the desk, pulled out the bottom drawer, and turned it over. From the bottom he pulled off the wood panel. In a secret space, there was one of the two handguns Jacob had brought back from Mexico in 2016. He pulled it out and loaded it with one mag and then took the second magazine and placed it in his pocket.

Trinity stepped from the bed and started to dress as fast as she could.

Four of the dark figures had made it up the long staircase and into the hall on the third floor. Slowly they moved down the hall, checking each bedroom on the floor, carefully opening each door.

As Trinity finished dressing, they thought they could hear movement just outside their door. They both stopped moving and froze. Jacob put his finger to his mouth, an indication for Trinity to be quiet.

Jacob slowly pulled the gun out, pulled the slide back, and released it, chambering a round in the gun. Then, as they watched, the door latch was lifted, and the door slowly swung open. The silenced barrel of a submachine gun started to appear. On the gun was a laser. The laser came on and swept across the room from right to left. Trinity froze in her tracks, not knowing what to do. Then the laser came across the bed and onto Trinity. She looked down at the laser dot on her chest in utter fear. The dark figure took one more step into the room. As it did, Jacob lifted the handgun and fired it four times, hitting the intruder. The figure fell back, and as it did, the submachine gun went off. Bullets flew past Trinity and hit the wall behind her. Stone chips went flying. Trinity dropped to the floor. Then a second figure stormed into the room, firing wildly. Bullets tore into the bed and the furniture around it. The gunman swung to the left, now firing at where Jacob was standing. The bullets shattered the window glass. Jacob dove for cover. As he did, he fired his gun at the attacker. He hid under the desk just as Trinity started to run across the room to the right. She dove over the bed and onto the floor on the far side. The gunman turned and fired at her. One round grazed her arm, and she yelled out in pain.

Jacob rolled over from behind the desk and found an opening to fire from between the two drawer stands. He pulled the trigger, firing twice, and the second round hit the figure in the head. The figure fell back, dropping to the floor.

The first shooter tried to stand again. The shooter was wearing body armor, and Jacob's bullets had only stunned it. Trinity rolled in pain on the floor, crying out; as she did, she saw a poker from the fireplace. She reached out and grabbed it, then rolled over. She stood and rushed toward the figure and hit it in the masked face with the poker. The figure dropped the gun and started to lash out at Trinity's assault, blocking her every move. It jumped to its feet and then kicked Trinity. She went flying to the floor. The figure then looked around for the gun, but as it did, it pulled out a knife and then stepped forward toward Trinity, the blade pointing at her.

Jacob stood up from behind the desk, drawing the gun. He aimed and fired, and one round hit the figure in the neck. The dark body dropped to the floor, choking for life.

Back in Tom and Keara's room, they were awoken by all the gunfire. Keara stood and grabbed a bathrobe. She put it on as Tom grabbed a shirt. He walked to the hall door and opened it. In the hall, in the dim light, he was just able to make out two shapes—bodies. Then, on this chest was a red laser dot. He looked down, but it was too late. A number of bullets went tearing through his body, knocking him back onto the floor. Keara saw his body fall. She screamed and rushed to Tom's side by the open door.

As she reached him lying on the floor, she screamed out, "*No!*"

Her arms went around him to hold him. As they did, she, too, was hit by gunfire from the hall attackers. Her body was thrown back; her face struck the cold floor. In her mind, the world was passing her by in slow motion. She looked across the now-blood-soaked floor and saw the lifeless face of Tom looking at her. She lay there. Then slowly her world drifted to black.

The two hooded hall figures now moved back down the hall toward the room of Trinity and Jacob.

Trinity slowly moved over to the struggling body of the shooter. Jacob made his advance, covering the shooter to make sure it no longer would threaten him or Trinity.

Trinity kneeled over the body fighting to live. She reached out and lifted the head of the shooter, then pulled off the black ski mask that hid the person's identity. From behind the blood-soaked mask was the face of a woman in her mid-twenties. She was Asian and in some ways reminded Trinity of Kim Wong, her long-lost friend. The memories of Kim's death on the ship came racing back to her. Trinity was in shock.

"My God!"

Jacob came and stood over the woman and looked down at her. He too was at a loss for words.

The woman looked at Trinity and reached her hand out to her as if asking for forgiveness. Trinity watched as the woman then drifted from this world to the next. Her head rolled sideways as she passed.

Trinity closed her eyes and lowered her head. Jacob came up behind her.

"Trinity, get up! There are more in the hall!" he whispered to her.

Jacob dropped the mag from the handgun, loaded his second fresh mag, and placed the used magazine in his pocket. He then slowly stepped over the two bodies and prepared to charge the hall. Trinity looked down and saw one of the assassin's guns. She picked up the submachine gun and stood up behind Jacob. There was a pause as he looked back to Trinity. He shook his head, as if to say, "Stay here."

He then lunged into the hall, firing the gun at the two attackers who approached. The black figures opened fire on Jacob, but missed him as he ran across the hall. Jacob hit one of the shooters in the leg, dropping him. At the same instant, Trinity ran forward and pointed the submachine gun into the hall, firing it wildly at the figures. The full-auto fire tore up the hall; wood and debris went flying. The second shooter dove for cover. Jacob had his chance. He dropped to one knee, fired at the fleeing figure, and hit him in the back and leg. The figure fell to the floor, sliding as he did. Trinity kept firing until the gun was empty.

Jacob then stood and walked down the hall, firing his gun at the two black figures lying on the floor. He hit each one several times, until his gun was empty and the slide locked back. Jacob stopped, dropped the empty mag, pulled out the half-used mag from before, and replaced it in the gun. He dropped the slide on the gun, chambering a round.

Jacob turned and called out to Trinity, "Come on!"

The two now started down the hall toward the stairs that led to freedom. As they did, a fifth figure came up from the shadow of the stairs and started to charge Jacob and Trinity. Trinity screamed out in fear. Jacob lifted the gun and fired at the attacker. The attacker opened fire on Trinity and Jacob. Bullets flew by in slow motion as Trinity dove for cover on the floor. Jacob was hit once, then a second time. But as he fell to his knees, he kept firing at the head of the shooter. The shooter's head went back, and he fell to the floor.

Jacob crashed to the floor; he tried to get up, but he couldn't. Trinity ran to his side and tried to help him to his feet.

"Get up!" she yelled at him. She put her arms around him and pulled at him, helped him to his feet, and then started to drag him down the hall toward the stairs.

As they arrived at the steps, the world around them suddenly exploded in gunfire. Bullets flew past them, tearing into the walls and ceiling. Plaster went flying everywhere. Trinity and Jacob fell to the floor to take cover.

A sixth shooter started up the staircase, firing his submachine gun toward where Trinity and Jacob were taking cover from the onslaught.

Trinity covered her face and head. She started to cry. As she lay there, she looked over to Jacob, who was now lying there, motionless, beside her. From the bottom of the stairs, the last two shooters now opened up on Trinity and Jacob, firing and then reloading and firing more. Trinity was pinned down. She could not move. Plaster and wood continued to rain down on her and Jacob.

As she lay there, she looked over to the dead gunman at the top of the stairs, the one Jacob shot in the head. On his chest were a set of futuristic-looking grenades. She looked back at Jacob, and then she turned and started to crawl over to the dead figure. Once there, she reached out and pulled two of the grenades from his vest and then slid sideways toward the railing of the stairs.

There she pulled the pin of each grenade and watched as the safety spoons flew off in slow motion. She then reached out and threw each of grenades over the side. The grenades fell to the main floor below. In Trinity's mind, the world was now almost standing still.

The grenades fell down, tumbling as they dropped, and finally hit the floor.

One of the masked shooters stopped firing and yelled out, "Grenade! Take cover!"

The figures turned to run, but it was too late. The first grenade went off, followed by the second one, a second later. The explosion was overwhelming. The force of the blast was so great, it tore through the centre of the stairwell and raced upward to the third floor. The shooter on the stairs was engulfed by fire and flying debris. The windows to one quarter of the house were blown out, sending glass flying out into the night sky.

Trinity covered her head and ears. As she did, she cried out, screaming for it to stop. Parts of the ceiling now came crashing down on her, just missing her. Fire was all around her, dancing in the night.

Slowly Trinity uncovered her face and started to stand. All around her was fire. It burned from below.

The sound of the Spanish house staff, running to help, could now be heard. They called out, "Fuego Fuego!" in Spanish.

Trinity crawled over to Jacob and turned his body over. She looked at him. He was still alive, but bleeding profusely.

"Jacob!" Trinity cried. "Don't die. Don't die. You can't die, not like this, not now, not here." She pulled his body close and held him as tight as she could.

From below, a number of Spanish housekeeping staff men entered the now-burning lower level of the house. They looked around the burning hall. Trinity cried out for help! The men heard her plea and then raced up the burning stairs to the third floor.

As they arrived, they found Trinity holding Jacob, crying. Two of the men leaned down, picked up Jacob, and started to carry him from the hall.

Trinity yelled out that Keara and Tom were still in their bedroom. Two more men ran past Trinity, toward Keara and Tom's room, passing over the two bodies in the hall. The men entered Keara and Tom's room and reached down, grabbed each of them, and started to carry them out.

The fire burned its way up the stairwell and now blocked their escape. From outside they could now hear the sound of bells ringing, letting the islanders know there was a fire and to send help.

From the third floor at the front of the house, they opened a window and started to climb onto the roof of the second story. They then made their way down to the second floor as more men arrived below.

The men worked as a team and helped lower them, one by one, to safety below. As they did, there were two more explosions from the stairwell as more grenades from the now-dead assassins exploded from the fire that burned around them. Part of the house now started to fall in on itself.

From the courtyard, Trinity stood looking back at the house as it burned. Wagons were brought in to take the four survivors to Trinity's old estate house next door. Men screamed in Spanish to hurry. Trinity finally looked down to her arm and saw the blood dripping from it to the cobblestone below. Each drop slowly splashed as it hit the stone. Then, as she stood there, the world around her started to spin around and around. She looked up to the night sky, now filled with the glow of burning sparks as they drifted slowly into heaven. Then the world turned to darkness as she fell to the ground.

Chapter Seventeen

Pain

October 21, 1882

Trinity awoke in a soft white bed surrounded by flowing white see-through drapes. She looked around and slowly stood up from bed. Her arm was bandaged, and her dress was white and clean. The light from the outside world blinded her. She looked around and slowly left the bed, placing one foot, then the other on the cool tile floor. Slowly she took her first step and then the next. She opened the door of the room and stepped into the hall. There in the hall was Carlos, the young man who first set eyes on her and the others when they first stepped foot in this time a year and a half ago.

Slowly Trinity walked down the hall toward him. Each step gave her more strength. She stopped in front of Carlos. "¿Dónde está Jacob y los demás?" Trinity said.

Carlos looked at her and then pointed for her to follow him. They walked down the hall to a side bedroom. The door swung open, and the two entered. In the room were two beds. In one was Jacob, and in the other was Keara.

A doctor wearing a white coat turned as they walked in. The older man looked over his glasses at her and said, "Es bueno verla caminando." He was glad to see Trinity walking.

Trinity walked into the room, toward the doctor. As she did, she looked over to Keara and stopped. She looked over at the doctor, hoping for some sign of how she was doing.

The doctor said in broken English, "She will be fine."

Trinity then turned and walked over to Jacob. She stopped and stood before his bed, gazing down at her husband. She looked up and over. The doctor stood next to her.

"How is he? Will he be all right?" Trinity asked.

"He will be all right; he will need time to heal. But he is strong; he has a will to live," the doctor told Trinity.

Trinity leaned down next to Jacob and looked at his face, then kissed him. She put her head on his chest. "Tom, where is Tom?"

The doctor turned and looked to the nurse who was standing nearby. Trinity lifted her head and looked over too.

Trinity walked into a dimly lit room on the first floor of the estate home. The only light was that of candles burning. There in the centre of the room was an open wood coffin. She slowly walked forward and stopped, looking down into it. There lying before her was her friend Tom. He looked so peaceful, at rest. Trinity stood there looking at him, her head tilted to one side as she smiled and tried once again to fight back the tears.

"I'm sorry. You were the one who was to live the longest. I'm sorry I took that away from you." Trinity bit her lip, closed her eyes, and started to weep. Tears streamed down her face. "Please forgive me; it wasn't supposed to end this way."

Carlos walked in and paused behind her. He wanted to step forward, but knew she needed to let go, to cry for her friend.

An hour later, Trinity walked into the horse stable of the estate with Carlos. Shafts of light crossed the dust-filled air. There, laid out, were eight bodies in different conditions of dismemberment. Some were badly burned; others were just as Trinity had last seen them. Three were women and five men. She slowly walked past their bodies and looked down at them. As she did, she studied each one. Unknown to Trinity, one of the men was the red-robed man from the future, his eyes still staring into space from when he died.

Carlos asked. "¿Quiénes eran?"

Trinity looked at him. "They were…people who believe everything has a place in time. Everything has an order."

Carlos asked, "What do we do with them?"

"Bury them. I don't care where." Trinity just continued to stand and look at them.

Then from the back of the stable, Maria could be heard. Trinity turned and looked back at her. She walked up beside Trinity, first looking at her and then down at the body-filled floor. She paused, then finally spoke.

"It is not safe, for you or for any of us."

Trinity stood there not saying anything.

"It is time to move on," Maria said.

Trinity slowly started to walk away, leaving the stable.

October 22, 1882

Keara cried in the arms of Trinity as she sat next her bed. Trinity held her, trying to give comfort to her in this time of need. As hard as she tried, she could not find the words to help her friend. She just sat there, holding her, placing her hand on her head.

October 23, 1882

It was just before midnight as Trinity sat in the bedroom, with Jacob in bed. The only light was from a single candle as she looked out to the sea. She then turned and looked back at Jacob, who was still sleeping. Her eyes went to the clock that sat on the mantel above the stone fireplace. The time was two minutes after midnight.

Trinity smiled. She had beaten the Grim Reaper for now.

I had survived. I had beaten death. What should have been the last day of my life had come and gone. I had proven that the past and the present are not connected. From this day forward, I would live my life not knowing what the last day would be. I would be free.

As I looked back at Jacob, I knew he would survive, as the doctor said he was strong. He would have too. Soon we would have to move on. Our place in this time was compromised. Somehow the Gatekeepers had found us.

I knew they would never stop until we were all dead. They had taken Tom, and for that I would never forgive this race of people from the future. There was only one place for us to go now. Perhaps we should have done it from the very first day we were given the chance. But now to survive, we would have no other choice.

Thank you, God, for giving me a future, for giving Keara a future, for giving Jacob a future. Please watch over Tom. Take care of him. And I hope he is with Robert, Kim, and Andy. I hope his children are by his side. I hope they are all together and looking down on us as they lift a glass of wine in our names.

I miss you all, my friends.

October 24, 1882

Trinity stood and looked on as the men came out of the ruins of the house carrying two wooden trunks from the basement cellar, one with the graphene computer and the other the field gate generators. They placed them at her feet.

Trinity looked at the men and then the trunks. The once-great estate home of Keara and Tom was now but a burned-out shell, a ruin of its former grandeur. The white walls were now charred and black, the roof was gone, and the trees around the house were burned to the ground.

Trinity kneeled down on the stone yard and placed her hands on each wooden trunk. She looked at them.

"Your job is not done," she said.

That afternoon, Trinity and Keara stood in the shared family tomb with a torch in Trinity's hand. They stood there looking at the now-sealed crypt of Tom.

"What date are you going to put?" Trinity asked.

"History said he died on April 12, 1780. Why change it?" Keara said.

Trinity then pulled Bianca's diary from a small bag she carried. She looked at it and then placed it into the open space that was to be her final resting place, her crypt, a dark, lonely place. Trinity stepped back as a man stepped up and placed the large stone that bore her name and date of death on it back over the tomb opening, sealing it.

"Good-bye Tom," Trinity said. She then turned and walked out of the tomb, leaving Keara standing there with the help of a set of crutches.

March 3, 1883

Trinity, Jacob, and Keara made the long march up the volcano, to the caves that brought them to this time two years earlier. Carlos stood watching them as they walked away, each carrying packs. In these packs were the computer and field gate generators, plus the food and water they would need as they waited.

Carlos called up to them one last time. "Good luck! It was, how you say, a pleasure knowing you, Great-Great-Great-Great-Grandmother."

Trinity turned and looked down at the young man. "Be safe. Live a long, happy life."

"You too," Carlos said, waving to them.

They entered the cave on March 3, 1883, and set up their equipment, like the times before, then waited for the moment in time that would take them across the next Rubicon.

Once the field gate generators were set, the three sat there looking at each other, the light from the lanterns casting long shadows on the cave walls. Trinity smiled at her friends. Jacob and Keara looked back at her, returning the smile. It wasn't a smile of joy; it was a token, a smile to mask their real feelings. They all felt great sadness. The last few years had been very hard on them.

Then the sound came, the taste.

"Wow, that was fast this time," Trinity said.

"Perhaps God has a place for us in our next stop," Keara said.

"Perhaps," Jacob said..

The area around them started to glow with the aurora of light. The light passed through them, and then they were gone.

Chapter Eighteen

The Gates of Olympus

October 17, 2016

The setting sun shone into their eyes as Trinity, Jacob, and Keara slowly walked down the winding road toward the gates of the Kennedy Warner Estate. They each carried a small backpack. The sea breeze swept back Trinity's hair as she walked with pride, her head high, a purpose in her stride.

Stopping at the massive 274-year-old wooden gates, the three travellers paused and looked at the sign that carried Jacob and Trinity's last names. Trinity turned and looked at Jacob and then Keara.

"Well?" Jacob said.

Trinity slowly stepped forward and pressed the intercom button next to the small wrought iron side-entry gate. As she did, she turned and looked back up over her shoulder, toward a video camera perched high above the gate that looked down on her. She waited. It seemed to take an eternity, when a voice finally came on.

"Hola, ¿la puedo ayudar?" came a female voice.

"Hello, we are…That is, we would like to see Maria Cruz and Carl Warner," Trinity replied.

There was a long pause and then in broken English: "They are busy and cannot see anyone!"

"Tell them Trinity would like to come home!" Trinity turned, looked up to the video camera, and smiled.

There was no sound or reply from the small speaker—just silence. Then, after what seemed to be forever, the sound of an older woman's voice could be heard.

"Who is this?" it demanded.

"Trinity."

There was a pause, then.

"Turn and look up at the camera!"

Trinity, Jacob, and Keara slowly turned and looked up at the small camera.

"Oh my God!" was the reply. "Trinity!"

Trinity smiled as she fought back the tears. "Hi, Mom. Please let us in."

"We are coming for you!" Maria called out.

With that, the wrought iron side gates buzzed open.

Jacob looked at Trinity. "After you."

Trinity pushed the gate open, and they all started to walk through. On the other side was the estate just as they had left it. If not for the streetlights that now lined the road, you would not have known the time in history.

Trinity, Jacob, and Keara slowly walked down the paved, tree-lined road toward the sound of the sea. As they walked, they could see off in the distance a white Suburban snaking its way toward them at high speed along the coastline.

Trinity reached out her hands and took the hand of Jacob to her right and Keara to her left. They walked hand in hand.

A journey was about to come to an end.

As the sun finally dipped into the sea, the SUV came over a small hill, slowed, and came to a stop in front of them. The three stopped and stood looking at the white SUV. The lights from the vehicle partially blinded them. Trinity lifted her hand to cover her eyes from the bright lights.

The doors to the SUV swung opened. Jacob and Keara turned and looked to Trinity.

I longed for years to see my mom and dad, my family, again. And with the grace of God, I was granted my wish. Miracles do happen. As I stand here tonight, I should be joyful, happy, and grateful.

But, all I can think about is when I was a child, so long ago, my father would say things to me, words, sayings, things that were meant to be lessons in life. At the time, I never gave him and his words much thought, always too busy with Facebook and my friends to care for him or my mother, but now, all these years later, as I stood here, his words came back to me so clearly. He once said to me, "When it comes to revenge, Trinity, revenge is a dish best served cold."

I looked forward to sharing my revenge with the help of my father. It would be a very cold revenge indeed, and I cherished it. I looked forward to it. I…We looked forward to paying the Gatekeepers a visit in 2337and returning the love they had shown to us.

From the shadows of the SUV stepped Maria, Carl, and Trinity's sisters, Ana and Bianca, into the light. There, standing before each of them, was their daughter, their sister Trinity. Not the Trinity of eighteen years, but the beautiful woman who Trinity became. They all slowly walked toward the three strangers.

Jacob looked to Keara and then to Trinity. "Semper Fi, Trinity." He gestured with his hands for Trinity to move forward to Maria, her mother.

Maria stopped and looked at Trinity. She slowly stepped forward, pausing, hesitating.

"Mom," Trinity said, fighting back her tears.

Maria put out her arms. Trinity dropped her backpack and ran towards them. They hugged, and each started to cry. The tears were from the soul. It hurt.

Carl walked up and put his arms around both of them. Then Ana and Bianca ran over, and they, too, tried to find a piece of her to hold.

Jacob and Keara looked on.

"Keara, Jacob, come here!" called Carl.

The two looked at each other, and they started to walk toward the group.

"You're home, my child. You are home." Maria fought to bring the words out as she held her daughter after so many years.

Carl put his head on Trinity as tears now rolled down his cheeks. "I looked for you."

"I love you…I love you," Trinity cried out. "I'm so sorry for never telling you that."

"You did, Trinity. You did," Maria cried.

With that ended the greatest journey of all time for three remarkable teens who had grown into remarkable adults. They started out as seven. Those who would not make it to the end would be missed and forever loved; their memory would always live on.

In the years ahead, Trinity, Jacob, and Keara, with the help of Carl Warner, would find their revenge on those who chose to take the life of Tom, on those who continued to seek to kill them. The cost would be high, but nothing in this world comes without sacrifice.

Tonight, for the first time in eighteen years, I am finally at peace. I once again have my family, my friends, my loved ones, and my husband by my side. Thank you, God. Thank you for letting me once again come home. Thank you for watching over me. Thank you for watching over my children for all the years I could not.

And finally, thank you that we are one again.

Semper Fi

The End

Toronto, Canada **2016**

Havana, Cuba **1755**

Santa Clara, Cuba **1755**

Puerto Maya, Mexico
2016 ≫ 1755

Chile Santiago
2016

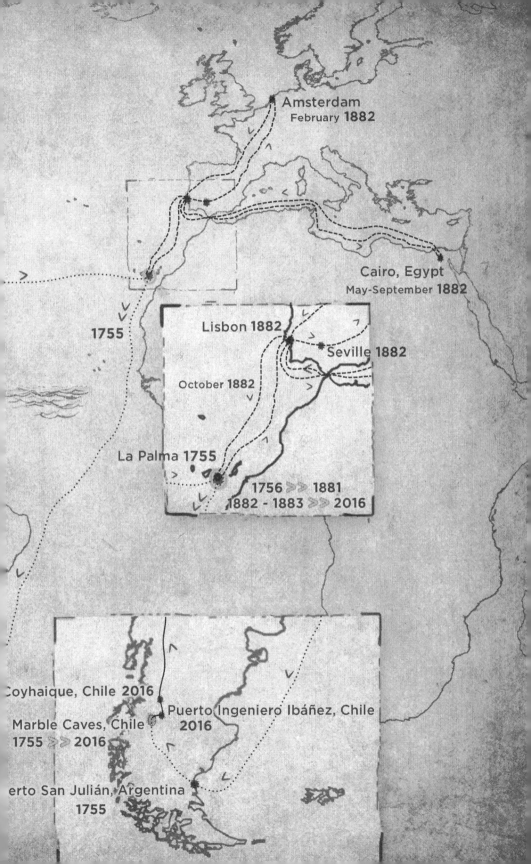

Amsterdam
February **1882**

Cairo, Egypt
May-September **1882**

1755

Lisbon 1882

Seville 1882

October 1882

La Palma 1755

1756 ≫ 1881
1882 - 1883 ≫ 2016

Coyhaique, Chile 2016

Marble Caves, Chile
1755 ≫ 2016

Puerto Ingeniero Ibáñez, Chile
2016

erto San Julián, Argentina
1755

R. C. Richter

Crossing the Rubicon III

"The Art of War"

Fall 2014

By

RC Richter

Made in the USA
Charleston, SC
12 February 2014